DOCTOR  WHO

Apollo 23

The DOCTOR WHO series from BBC Books

DOCTOR WHO

Apollo 23

JUSTIN RICHARDS

1 3 5 7 9 10 8 6 4 2

First published in 2010 by BBC Books, an imprint of Ebury Publishing.
A Penguin Random House Group Company.
This edition published in 2015.

The Random House Group Limited Reg. No. 954009

Addresses for companies within the Random House Group can be found at:
www.randomhouse.co.uk

A CIP catalogue record for this book is available from the British Library.

ISBN 9781849909730

Commissioning editor: Albert DePetrillo
Series consultant: Justin Richards
Editor: Stephen Cole
Project editor: Steve Tribe
Cover design: Lee Binding © Woodlands Books Ltd, 2010
Production: Rebecca Jones

Penguin Random House is committed to a sustainable future
for our business, our readers and our planet. This book is
made from Forest Stewardship Council® certified paper.

Printed and bound in Great Britain by Clays Ltd, St Ives PLC

To buy books by your favourite authors and register for offers,
visit www.randomhouse.co.uk

For Jim, Nick, & Simon –
the Gentlemen who Lunch

Twenty minutes before he died, Donald Babinger was feeding bits of his cheese sandwich to a pigeon.

It was a cold, grey day, and the pigeon seemed grateful for the attention as well as the crumbs. It pecked eagerly at the bread, ignoring the cheese and the pickle. Babinger was sitting on the steps up to the bandstand, huddled in his coat. The bandstand was where the teenagers hung out in the evening, in the park near the library. The railings were rusted and the pitted concrete floor was studded with dark blobs of well-trodden chewing gum. But the cracked roof offered some shelter from the persistent drizzle.

Ten minutes before he died, Donald Babinger stuffed the last remains of his sandwich into his mouth, smiled apologetically at the pigeon, and stood up. A brisk walk round the edge of the little park, then back to the office. He liked to get out at lunchtime, even when the weather wasn't so good.

Babinger believed it was a good idea to get a breath of fresh air.

Which was ironic, given how he was about to die.

His mind already returning to the spreadsheet he needed to sort out in the afternoon, Babinger walked slowly across the little park. He nodded a mute greeting to a young woman pushing a toddler in a buggy. He smiled at a woman in a red raincoat walking her dog. He shook his head sadly at the litter blown in clusters against the low metal fence round a flowerbed. He wondered yet again how the developers ever got permission for the new shopping centre that cast its grey concrete and glass shadow across the end of the park. His colleague Mandy would still be queuing for her lunch at Perfect Burger. What a waste of time when you could bring your own sandwich...

Perhaps he wouldn't have begrudged her the time if Babinger knew he only had five minutes left to live.

He spent most of that five minutes completing his tour of the park. With only thirty seconds left to live, he checked his watch, saw that his lunch break was almost over, and turned back towards the bandstand. The mother and toddler were on the other side of the park. There was no sign of the woman with the dog.

Babinger decided to cut across the park rather than follow the path the rest of the way. Best to get back and crack on with the accounts. Yes, that was the wise decision.

The decision that killed him.

Donald Babinger was almost back at the bandstand

when he felt the first tightness in his chest, the first difficulty in getting his breath. His vision blurred and swam. He blinked, and shook his head to clear it. But the world was going grey. The sky was darkening.

His breathing came in ragged gasps. His chest continued to tighten. The ground under his feet was no longer damp grass but dry dust. The shopping centre was gone. The bandstand was gone. Everything was gone, and in its place…

'Oh my—' Babinger started to say.

But no words came.

He had no breath to speak them.

Babinger was on his knees, his hands tearing at his burning throat. His tongue fizzed like his saliva was boiling. His eyes felt like they were about to burst. Babinger's whole body seemed light and bloated. He fell onto his back, convulsing and shaking. So *cold*.

Then, abruptly, he was still. The drizzle pattered on his face. It pooled into his unseeing eyes, until it overflowed and ran gently down his face like tears.

'We'll need a post mortem, of course,' the pathologist said.

The police sergeant nodded. He waited for the photographer to finish, then gestured to the waiting ambulance crew.

'You can take him away now. Poor bloke.' He turned to the pathologist. 'So, what do you reckon?'

Dr Winterbourne shrugged. He had worked with the police for over twenty years – long enough to know not to commit himself, but also to be aware that sometimes a quick diagnosis could be vital. 'Probably heart failure. He seems healthy enough, apart from being dead of course, but you can never tell. Just because he looks young and fit…' He sighed. 'There's no justice in the world.'

Sergeant Rickman suppressed a grin. 'Thanks for that.'

'I mean, not in this sort of thing.'

'I know.'

They both watched solemnly as the ambulance men drew a dark plastic sheet over the body on the stretcher.

'Yes, must have been his heart,' Winterbourne decided. 'Though it's funny – the colour of his skin, the way his tongue…' His voice tailed off. 'Well, it's all consistent with asphyxiation. As though he were strangled.'

'He was on his own,' Rickman said flatly. 'That woman with the kid saw him from over by the gates. Said he just sort of clutched his face and then keeled over. She'd just taken the kid out of his buggy, so she couldn't leave him and run over to help. Shouted the place down till someone else noticed.'

The ambulance pulled away into the traffic. A small group of people stood on the other side of a taped boundary, watching. A reporter from the local paper waved a notepad and tried to catch the sergeant's eye.

'Let me know about the post mortem,' the policeman said. 'For now let's say it seems like natural causes, no suspicious circumstances. That sound OK to you?'

'Fine, fine,' Winterbourne agreed. 'You know,

there's a little Italian place up there.' He pointed at the curved glass wall of the looming shopping centre.

'You're thinking there might be other witnesses?'

'I'm thinking I've not had any lunch,' Winterbourne corrected him. 'Talk to you later.'

Mandy had been queuing at Perfect Burger for ten minutes when the spaceman appeared.

They didn't just do burgers. She usually had a tuna salad, which was a bit more healthy. With chips. But today was so cold and grey she didn't really fancy salad. She was looking at the menu board when the spaceman arrived.

One moment he wasn't there, the next he was. Maybe she blinked. He must have stepped out from the door to the toilets or something. Funny she'd missed that – a figure so bulky in a white spacesuit and bulbous helmet couldn't just appear.

He stood staring at Mandy. Or she imagined he did. She couldn't see his face, because the helmet was a gold-tinted mirror that reflected the queue of people as more and more of them slowly turned to look.

The astronaut moved awkwardly in his spacesuit. He walked stiffly towards Mandy, swaying from side to side – his legs didn't seem to bend enough to move easily.

When he was so close she could have reached out and touched him, the spaceman stopped. There was a trail of fine grey dust across the floor behind him. His large boots were coated in it, Mandy saw. The trail stopped by the menu board – like he really had just appeared there.

'Must be a publicity thing,' someone behind Mandy said.

'Selling something, yeah,' a man agreed. 'He's going to tell us he's just had the greatest pizza in the solar system, or something.'

The queue wasn't really a queue any longer. Everyone was gathering round the spaceman. People were coming over from the other fast food outlets. Shoppers on the gallery above were staring down, pointing and laughing. As publicity stunts went, this one seemed to be working.

The spaceman lifted his arms, reaching up to fumble with the clamps at the point where the suit joined the helmet.

'Bet he's hot in that.'

'What's he advertising anyway? Some new movie, d'you think?'

There was a hiss of pressurised air as the clamps released. The astronaut twisted the helmet sideways. Then he lifted it off his head.

Beneath the helmet, the man was wearing a white hood, like a balaclava. There was what looked like a phone headset attached, complete with earpiece and microphone. He looked even more awkward holding the helmet, and instinctively Mandy reached out to take it from him.

'Thank you, ma'am.' He had a deep voice, with an American accent. Mandy could now see there was a small US flag on his shoulder, and under it his name, she assumed – GARRETT.

His hands now free, the astronaut pulled off the hood, to reveal dark, close-cropped hair beneath. He looked to be in his thirties, with eyebrows that almost met in the middle above his wide nose. He untangled the headset from the hood and glared at it in evident frustration.

'Anyone here got a cell phone I can loan?'

The man behind Mandy laughed. 'I've got a *mobile* you can *borrow*.'

'You're not in Kansas any more,' someone else called.

'Yeah, I guessed.' Astronaut Garrett smiled thinly, but Mandy could see the concern and worry in his grey eyes, the way he swayed unsteadily on his feet, as he took the man's mobile.

For a moment, he stared at the small buttons on the mobile and then the broad, stumpy fingers of his glove.

'Want me to dial?' Mandy asked. She offloaded the helmet to another woman, then took the phone. She punched in the number the astronaut told her. It started 001 – wasn't that the code for the USA? Mandy was glad it wasn't going on *her* bill.

'It's ringing.' She handed it back.

The phone disappeared inside the enormous gloved palm. Garrett raised it to his ear. There was silence as everyone waited to hear who he was talking to. Waited for some clue as to what he might be selling or promoting.

In the middle of the silent shopping centre, right outside Perfect Burger, Garrett's voice was clear.

'Houston,' he said, 'we have a problem.'

Chapter

1

The lunchtime rush was almost over, and there were a few spaces left in the car park.

A sudden breeze stirred the autumn leaves, whirling them into an unnatural frenzy. A rasping, grating sound split the air. With a resolute concluding 'thump', a dark blue police telephone box stood solidly where it had not been a few moments earlier. It straddled two of the parking spaces, the light on top flashing for a moment.

Almost at once, the doors of the TARDIS opened and the Doctor strode out. He looked round with interest at the parked cars. He glanced up at the grey sky. He blinked rain out of one eye, and he flicked his head to get his damp hair out of the other. Then he straightened his bow tie and pulled his crumpled jacket into some semblance of order.

'Great,' Amy said, stepping out behind him. The breeze blew her long red hair round her face. 'The planet Car-Park, one of the most glamorous locations in the Asphalt Galaxy.'

The Doctor nodded in full agreement. 'Though actually,' he said, 'it could be Earth. Britain at an expert guess.'

'You got that from the car number plates,' Amy said.

'No. From the weather. Look at that.' The Doctor held his hand out to let the light rain moisten it.

'I do recognise rain,' Amy told him. 'I'm Scottish, remember?' She fumbled in her jeans pockets. 'Got any money?'

'Tons.'

'I mean *money* money. Like change. For the machine.'

The Doctor stared at her blankly.

'Never mind.' Amy had found a pound coin and a few ten pence pieces.

The Doctor watched with interest as she fed them into the nearest ticket machine, then pressed a big green button.

'What are you doing?'

'Ticket,' she said, as it printed out and dropped into a little slot at the bottom of the machine. 'It's pay and display.'

'Display what?'

'The ticket.'

Amy ducked back into the TARDIS, and stuck the ticket inside the bottom of one of the windows in the door.

'We're staying then?' the Doctor said as she came out and closed the doors. He nodded at the ticket visible through the glass.

'Only for a couple of hours. That's all I could afford.'

'And what are we doing?'

Amy led the way towards a large building that looked like it had been thrown together out of glass and concrete.

'Shopping.'

The Doctor nodded, wrinkling his nose against the thin rain. 'The whole universe,' he announced as they entered the concrete and glass shopping arcade. 'All of time and space. From the creation of Bandrazzle Maxima to the heat-death of Far-Begone. From the tip of Edgewaze to the Bakov Beyonned... And you want to go shopping.'

A little old lady with a walking stick turned to look at him suspiciously. The Doctor grinned at her and said 'Hello'. She moved quickly on.

'Nothing wrong with a bit of a shop. It's got to be done. We can have lunch too,' Amy added, pointing to a clock mounted on the wall nearby.

'Lunch?' The Doctor sucked in his cheeks and stuffed his hands into his jacket pockets. 'Well that's all right then. I haven't had lunch for centuries.'

There was a little Italian restaurant on the first floor. Amy chose a table close to the large window looking out onto a small park with a bandstand in the middle. She could also see down to the floor below where people were queuing for burgers and other fast food.

The Doctor inspected the plasticised menu that was left propped up between the salt and pepper.

'Do they come to us or do we have to go to them?' he wondered. 'I can't see milk mentioned.'

'They must have it for the coffee. Unless they use those little pots.'

'I bet they use those little pots.' The Doctor leaned back in his chair, tilting it dangerously, long fingers laced together behind his head. 'Do they come to us or do we go to them?' he asked loudly. 'To order, I mean?'

It took Amy a moment to realise he was talking not to her, but to the man at the table behind him. The man was wearing a dark, crumpled suit and looked about 50 years old with greying hair.

Getting no answer, the Doctor somehow managed to turn the chair, pivoting it on one leg so he was sitting facing the man across his table.

'Oh, sorry,' the man said. 'Yes, they come to you. Well, they came to me.' He smiled across at Amy and the Doctor. 'But maybe I'm special.'

'Everyone's special,' the Doctor told him. 'Look at Amy, she's *really* special. And I'm the Doctor.' He stuck his hand out.

The man politely half stood as they shook hands. 'Me too.'

The Doctor's brow creased into a slight frown. 'Small universe.' He nodded at the man's plate of pasta. 'You're not eating much. Is the food here rubbish, then?'

'No, no. It's very good.' The man poked at the pasta with his fork. 'But I do find death rather spoils my appetite.'

The Doctor sighed. 'I know the feeling. Mind you,

I haven't died for months. Quite hungry afterwards, I find.' He swung the chair back to face Amy. 'Probably means he's vegetarian or something. Bit of a weird way of saying it.'

Amy wasn't sure that was what the man had meant at all. She got up and went to sit in the spare chair at the man's table.

'You said "me too". Do you mean you're a doctor?'

'Yes. Well, pathologist, actually. Gyles Winterbourne.'

The Doctor had spun back again. 'Ah – hence the death.'

Winterbourne turned to the large window beside them. 'This probably wasn't the best place to sit. The poor chap died down there, in the park.'

'Accident?' Amy asked. She could see several policemen standing round and a small group of onlookers.

'Natural causes.' He hesitated before adding: 'I think.'

'You're not sure?' the Doctor prompted.

'Need to do a post mortem. Something else to put you off your food.' Winterbourne stabbed at a tube of pasta, lifted it to his mouth, then changed his mind and put the loaded fork back into the bowl. 'You're a doctor, you ever seen a case of heart failure with all the symptoms of asphyxiation?'

The Doctor blew out a long breath as he considered. 'Well, I'm not actually a medical doctor.'

'Student?' Winterbourne suggested.

Amy stifled a smile as the Doctor glared at the

other man, affronted. 'I've seen more death than you've avoided hot dinners.'

'And then there's the dust,' Winterbourne went on, almost to himself. 'Gets everywhere – look, there's still some on my sleeve.' He turned his cuff to show a pale grey spattering of dry dust.

The Doctor's frown returned. He grabbed Winterbourne's hand and pulled it across the table so suddenly the man almost went face-down in his pasta. Then, just as abruptly, he let go again.

'Sorry,' Amy said.

Winterbourne smiled weakly back at her. 'There's loads of it down by the burger place,' he said. 'If dust is your thing.'

'The burger place?' the Doctor asked, turning to look.

'Downstairs. You know, where the spaceman is.'

'Figures,' the Doctor said dismissively, and picked up the menu. 'After all, it is moon dust.'

Amy watched the Doctor and mentally counted off the seconds. She got to four.

The Doctor dropped the menu and leaped to his feet. 'Hang on, hang on. Moon dust – in a shopping centre? And a spaceman?'

'Well, an astronaut. Publicity stunt, or so someone said.' Winterbourne pointed. 'Look, there he is now, with those men in suits.'

The chair the Doctor had been sitting on crashed to the floor. Startled, Winterbourne turned to Amy. But she too had gone.

She was following the Doctor rapidly across to the other side of the restaurant. Together they leaned on the railing, looking down at the fast food outlets on the floor below.

'Astronaut,' Amy said. 'He'll be the one in the spacesuit, I bet.' The astronaut was walking stiffly across the shopping centre, carrying his bulbous helmet under one padded arm. 'It's a good costume.'

'It's not a costume,' the Doctor said.

Amy pointed to the three men is dark suits, all wearing sunglasses and unnecessarily short haircuts. 'And those aren't American Secret Service Agents either.'

The Doctor sighed. 'Amy Pond.'

'Sorry.'

'They're with the CIA.'

They watched in silence as the men in suits led the astronaut out of the arcade. Moments later, a large, black car with darkened windows drove past the little park.

'So, what have we got here?' Amy asked, leaning back against the rail, legs stretched out. 'Astronaut who's stopped off for a burger, or what?'

'Moon dust... astronaut...' The Doctor pushed himself away from the railing. 'And asphyxiation. The dead man had dust on him – come on!'

Amy had to run to catch up as the Doctor hurried towards the nearest escalator. She'd been looking forward to a bit of shopping. It would have been so ordinary after what she'd experienced recently. Now it looked like ordinary wasn't on the menu after all.

'Where are we going?'

'Back to the TARDIS. If I'm right...' He paused, mid-step, and pulled out his sonic screwdriver.

'I'm right,' he confirmed after a moment. 'Quantum displacement.' Then he was off again.

'And what is quantum displacement, when it's at home?' Amy asked on the escalator.

'Serious. And it isn't at home – that's the point. It's been displaced. Like the astronaut, and the dead man.'

He was standing beside a police box in the car park, wearing a dark blue uniform, but he wasn't a policeman. The parking warden checked the ticket showing through the window of the TARDIS, and made a note on his pad. He checked his watch and made another note.

'Problem?' Amy asked brightly.

The warden sniffed. 'Problem,' he agreed.

'We're well within the time,' Amy told him.

'We are,' the Doctor agreed, leaning over to see what the man was writing. 'I'm an expert. I know all about time.'

'Time's not an issue.'

'Well, you say that,' the Doctor replied. 'But actually...'

'So what is the problem?' Amy asked before he could go on.

The parking warden pointed to the ticket in the window. Then he pointed at the ground, where the TARDIS stood. 'One ticket. Two spaces.'

Amy's eyes narrowed. 'You're not serious.'

'He looks serious,' the Doctor said.

'You have to park within spaces,' the warden said.

'But we're too big,' the Doctor explained. 'Look – narrow space, wide box. It won't fit.'

'Then you need two tickets. One for each space. If you want to dump some antique like that in a car park, you have to pay for the spaces. Sooner you get it towed away again, the better.'

'So you're going to give us a fine?' Amy asked.

'Not me. The council will give you the fine. I just issue the bill. Fifty quid.'

'Fifty?' the Doctor was already reaching inside his jacket.

Amy glared at him. 'We're not paying fifty quid.'

The warden shrugged. 'Then it'll be a hundred. If you don't pay within twenty-four hours, that is.'

The Doctor removed his hand from inside his jacket. He was holding a plain leather wallet. 'Wait, wait, wait. I can settle this.'

'Put the money in the machine,' the warden said. 'Send the ticket it gives you to the council and they'll accept that as payment.'

'Like we have fifty pounds in coins in our pockets,' Amy said.

The Doctor flipped open his wallet to reveal what Amy knew was a blank sheet of psychic paper. It would show whatever the person looking at it expected or was persuaded to see.

'Two-for-one voucher,' the Doctor announced. 'Look – here you go. That should sort it out. The bearer has the right to one free car-park ticket for every ticket purchased at full price. Second ticket need not be displayed. See, it says so right here. Authorised by the district council.'

The warden frowned. 'Let me see that.' He took the psychic paper from the Doctor and examined it carefully. 'Yes, well that seems to be in order,' he muttered glumly.

The Doctor grinned at Amy.

'You should have shown me this straight away,' the warden said. 'Would have saved a lot of bother.'

'Yeah. Sorry. Can I have it back now?' The Doctor held out his hand.

'In a moment.' The warden licked the end of his pen. He teased the sheet of paper out from behind the protective plastic window of the wallet. 'Just need to sign this to authorise it.'

The Doctor's eyes widened. But the man was already signing his name across the paper before sliding it back, snapping the wallet shut and handing it back. 'There you go, sir.' He touched the peak of his uniform cap with his hand. 'Miss. Mind how you go.'

'He *signed* it,' the Doctor said in a harsh whisper after the warden had gone. Then louder: 'He *signed* it. He *signed* my psychic paper.' He opened the wallet and stared in disbelief. '"Albert Smoth", is that? I can't even read it. He's ruined my psychic paper.'

'Oh, get over it,' Amy said. 'Saved us fifty quid, didn't it? Give it here.' She took the wallet, and slid out the paper, then turned it over and slid it back into place, the blank, unsigned side now visible through the plastic window.

The Doctor took the wallet back. 'Yeah, OK. That'll work,' he admitted. 'Probably.'

*

'That was quick,' Amy said, a few minutes later.

'No time at all.' The Doctor pushed home a lever on the TARDIS console. 'Really, no time at all. I just removed the safeties, drifted a bit to the west in the fourth dimension, and let the TARDIS fall through the quantum displacement. It's closed up now, of course, so she had to jig back in time a bit, then edge forwards again to compensate.'

'So where are we?'

The Doctor opened the doors, and they both turned to see.

Amy gasped. 'It's amazing. So desolate, but so beautiful.' She started down the slope towards the doors.

'Don't go out,' the Doctor warned. 'There's just a force membrane keeping the air inside the TARDIS. Pass through it and you'll suffocate in seconds. Like the man Dr Winterbourne was telling us about.'

Amy turned back to the Doctor. 'Is that what happened? He got, like, *displaced*?'

The Doctor walked slowly down to join her near the doors. 'He was in the park, and he was also here. The two places are joined by the displacement process, so you can walk from one into the other. Except the overlap is unstable. Something's gone wrong. For a while, maybe just a minute or two, he was *here*.'

'And the astronaut?'

'Same thing, only the other way round. And more permanent. He walked from here into the shopping centre. If the displacement had stayed open he could have turned round and walked back again.'

'From Earth to the moon,' Amy murmured. 'Talk

about a giant step for mankind.'

They both stared out across the empty grey craters of the dark side of the moon.

Chapter
2

General Adam Walinski stared out across the empty waste of the desert. It stretched as far as he could see. Only the fenced compound round Base Hibiscus broke the grey-yellow of the sand.

A shadow fell across the wide window behind his desk. Walinski didn't turn.

'How can this happen, Candace?' he asked, his Texan accent drawing out the vowels. 'They said it was impossible for anything to go wrong. *You* said so.'

'Seems I was mistaken. Big time. The pictures from Base Diana are coming through now.'

Now Walinski did turn. He stared down at the slight figure of Dr Candace Hecker. Somehow, despite her khaki military uniform, she still managed to look like a civilian. Her shoulder-length brown hair was hanging loose, and the top button of her tunic was undone. Walinski didn't look at her boots, but he knew that they wouldn't be polished.

'Do I want to see the pictures?' he demanded.

She shrugged. 'I do. Like you said, something's gone wrong. Maybe the pictures will tell us what. Sir,' she added as an afterthought.

The first of the photographs was coming off the printer in Hecker's office when they got there. It showed the body of a woman in a red coat. Several of Hecker's staff were gathered round. Graham Haines lifted the print, still damp, from the printer's output tray and laid it on Hecker's desk for everyone to see.

'Obviously a major malfunction,' Haines said.

'Becky Starmer,' Candace said. 'Thirty-four years old. No kids, which I guess is a mercy. Husband says she went out every lunchtime to walk the dog. Even when it was raining – which it was at the time of the, uh, incident.'

'What time was Garrett's call?' Walinski asked.

'17.32,' someone replied.

Walinski jabbed his finger at the woman in the photo. 'And this happened…?'

'She was spotted at 17.53 our time,' Hecker told him. 'Major Carlisle got anxious when Garrett didn't report in on the half-hour. She went to look for herself from the Section 4 observation gallery.'

'And the photos?' Walinski asked, as Haines laid a second damp print beside the first picture.

'About ten minutes later. Colonel Devenish scrambled a team from Base Diana to recover the bodies.'

'Bodies – *plural*?' Walinski said.

In answer, Haines put another photograph down on the desk.

Walinski stared at the pictures and shook his head. 'She's got a *dog* – can this get any worse?'

A man at the back of the group cleared his throat. He was wearing a dark suit – not military. 'The dog's called Poochie,' he said. 'The agents in England who collected Garrett interviewed the woman's husband. And the colleagues of the Babinger guy too. Their report's just come through.'

'Hooray for the CIA,' Walinski muttered. Louder he said: 'Thank you, Agent Jennings. Anything else you can tell us? Preferably about Poochie's owner, not his pedigree.'

Agent Jennings eased his way to the front of the group. There were now three pictures on the desk. He pointed to the first, which showed a woman lying on her side. Her blonde hair was splayed out around her head. Her damp, red raincoat was spattered with grey dust. Jennings tapped the second photo – a close-up of a small white dog with dark markings. The dog was also lying on its side, mouth open, eyes wide.

'Poor old Poochie,' Jennings said with no sincerity. 'They say dogs look like their owners, don't they?'

The third photo was a close-up of the woman's head, the hair like a halo on the dark ground.

'She had her roots done a couple of days ago,' Jennings said, 'so I guess she's looking her best.'

'Aside from being dead,' Walinski said.

'Aside from that.'

They all stared at the photos. Becky Starmer's red coat was like a splash of blood – the strongest colour, distinct and out of place against the grey of the background.

The grey of the dark side of the moon.

Where Becky Starmer and her little dog lay frozen and dead at the edge of a crater.

'You know,' Candace Hecker said quietly, 'for a few moments this afternoon, it actually rained on the moon. Just like it did in England...'

A little later, Hecker and Walinski sat on opposite sides of the General's desk. The photos lay discarded between them.

'Captain Garrett's on his way here now,' Hecker said.

'Maybe he can tell us why we're up the creek without a parachute,' Walinski said.

'Let's hope someone can. We're down to bouncing radio signals off the satellites. There's a time delay of nearly a minute and the bandwidth is rubbish.'

'Why now?' Walinski asked. 'The system's worked for over thirty years. Why's it suddenly gone to pieces?'

Hecker shook her head. 'I'm the most experienced technician here, and I don't understand how it works when everything's running fine,' she confessed. 'The equipment's well maintained. The components are switched out regularly. Professor Jackson up on Diana tells us they've replaced all the major equipment and it still isn't working. Anyway, with a blow-out it'd just stop. Not this.' She leaned forward and pointed to the picture of Becky Starmer dead on the moon. 'And not Marty Garrett suddenly finding himself in a shopping mall in England.'

Walinski nodded. 'Hell, the desert out there I could

understand.' He waved a hand over his shoulder, indicating the window behind him. 'But England? What the hell's *that* all about?'

There was a knock at the door. Walinski called out permission to enter. Agent Jennings opened the door.

'Video feed's online. They're recovering the woman's body. And the dog. If you want to see?'

'Not likely to tell us much,' Walinski said. 'But it's better than sitting around here.'

'What's the delay on the link?' Hecker asked.

'A minute or so, apparently,' Jennings said.

'What's the problem?' Walinski asked.

'Real time went out with the quantum displacement,' Hecker explained. 'The radio waves actually have to come all the way from the moon now, not just across the desert.'

There was a group of people already gathered round a large flat-panel monitor on the other side of the open-plan office area. They parted respectfully to allow Walinski and Hecker a better view. Jennings kept out of the way – an outsider in this close-knit community under pressure.

The colour was washed out, and the picture was grainy and juddered. It showed several astronauts, dressed in the same bulky white suits as Garrett had worn when he appeared outside Perfect Burger. They bounced and lurched in a slightly ungainly manner as they busied themselves round the red stain on the image that was Becky Starmer's coat.

The image changed as the astronaut holding the camera turned. For a moment, the screen showed the dull grey expanse of the moon, unbroken for as far as the eye could see. Then it spun again, and Becky was being lifted onto a stretcher.

No one spoke as they watched the astronauts place the dog next to its late mistress. Two of the suited figures lifted the stretcher and started across the empty landscape.

The picture lurched and spun again as the astronaut holding the camera moved to follow them. A glimpse of desolation. Then, in the distance, the low box-shaped, modular buildings that made up the outer sections of Base Diana.

'Hang on,' Hecker said. 'Can you rewind?'

'We're streaming it to DVD,' Haines said. 'It'll take me a minute, but we can view the recording rather than the live feed.'

'What is it?' Walinski asked. 'What did you see?'

'Maybe nothing,' Hecker conceded. 'Just a flash of colour. Something that seemed out of place. I just want to see what it was.'

A few moments later, the science team, Walinski and Agent Jennings regarded the frozen image on the monitor in collective astonishment.

'Rewind further,' Jennings said. He pushed his way through the group. 'The guy with the camera turned that way about a minute before. Show us that.'

Haines worked the mouse, and the computer ran the DVD-recorded images backwards rapidly.

'I don't know what's more worrying,' Walinski said at last. He pointed to the screen, showing the empty, grey desolation of the moonscape. 'The fact that a large blue box is standing exactly where it shouldn't be on the moon within sight of Base Diana…'

'Or the fact that it wasn't there a minute before,' Hecker finished for him.

'Whatever it is,' Jennings said quietly, 'I advise you to get a recovery team out there right away.'

Walinski turned to look at the man in the suit. 'That's what you *advise*, is it?'

Jennings raised his eyebrows. 'Only a suggestion, General. Hey – I'm just an observer. You're in charge here, you know.'

The way he said it left no one in any doubt who was really in charge.

General Walinski turned to Haines. 'Get a recovery team out to that blue box. Right now.'

Chapter
3

The look of surprise on the man's face made it worth it. Amy didn't like the spacesuit. It was tight in all the wrong places, the helmet was claustrophobic – like someone had stuck a goldfish bowl over her head. She could hear her own breathing, and the whole thing was just not quite her shade of red.

It didn't help that the Doctor's voice was an enthusiastic blast in her ears and she didn't know how to turn the volume down. Either the suit volume, or the volume of the Doctor's excitement as he bounced happily across the barren lunar surface.

But it was all worth it when she was standing beside the Doctor, at the edge of a crater, behind a man in a bulky white suit.

The Doctor reached out and tapped the man on the shoulder. He turned slowly, clumsily, in little hopping movements. His eyes were already wide and anxious through the faceplate. When he saw the Doctor and

Amy standing there, the man took a step backwards and almost fell. His eyebrows shot upwards, as if to escape from his jaw as it dropped in the opposite direction.

'Whoa – where did you come from?' an American voice gasped in Amy's ear.

The Doctor gestured vaguely back over his shoulder.

Amy grinned.

'Is there another base?' The man shook his head inside his helmet, which didn't move. 'No, no way. We'd know.'

'Just visiting,' the Doctor told him. Amy could see from his expression that the man could hear. The Doctor must have opened their radio link to include him. 'I gather you're having a problem with your quantum displacement.'

'You're from Hibiscus?'

'Well, we're from TARDIS actually. But we can sort that out inside.'

'So what are you up to?' Amy asked, as much to prove she could speak as anything. 'Just getting some air?'

'Recovery team.'

He turned in cumbersome bouncing steps. Maybe this spacesuit wasn't so bad after all, Amy decided. It certainly seemed easier to move in it, and the whole thing was much less bulky.

'Recovery,' the Doctor said. 'You been ill? Some sort of therapy?'

'We recover stuff from outside, from here on the surface. Equipment, monitoring systems, solar panels that need replacing. Sometimes just rocks for Jackson's people to examine'

'And today?' Amy asked.

The man paused in his bouncing, lolloping walk. He half turned, then seemed to decide it was too much effort and started bouncing off again.

'Today,' he said, 'we were recovering the body.'

They crested a shallow rise in the ground – the lip of another enormous crater, Amy realised. Ahead of them the ground sloped away again – towards a cluster of low, rectangular buildings connected by even lower, rectangular corridor sections. The whole thing looked like it had been made out of enormous egg boxes for some children's school project.

Just a short way ahead of them were several more astronauts in identical bulky white suits. Two of them carried a stretcher. Amy couldn't make out the detail of what was on it – just a splash of bright red, incongruous against the grey of the moon's surface.

'Who was she?' the Doctor asked. His eyesight must be better.

'Don't know yet. Some poor woman and her dog. They walked right through the displacement field, and wound up here. Dead. Suffocated in moments.'

'Like that poor guy in the park,' Amy said.

'The field must have dissipated round him,' the Doctor said thoughtfully. 'That poor woman walked right into it. A walk in the park becomes a moonwalk.'

'And we lost Marty Garrett.'

'Guessing he was the guy who walked off the moon into the burger bar,' Amy said.

'Seems likely,' the Doctor agreed.

They walked on in silence for several minutes. As they got closer, Amy could see that the moonbase in front of them was much larger than she had thought. The box-like modules rose high above them like office blocks.

'It's so big,' she said.

'Most of it will be storage,' the Doctor told her. 'Water, air, food, that sort of thing.'

'Thank goodness,' the astronaut said. 'They were talking a couple of years ago about just piping water and air in direct from Base Hibiscus and not storing anything locally. If they'd done that we'd be working out whether we die of thirst before oxygen starvation, now the quantum link's gone down.'

'The thing that lets you walk from Earth to the moon,' Amy said.

'Or pipe water and air though,' the astronaut said. 'Luckily the tanks have been kept full through the quantum link and the underground reservoir. We should be OK for three months. You'll have it fixed by then, right?'

He sounded like he was joking. The Doctor didn't answer.

'So where's the Earth?' Amy asked, changing the subject. 'Shouldn't we be able to see it?'

'This is the dark side of the moon,' the Doctor told her.

'But it isn't dark.'

'It's *called* the dark side. That's not because it's actually dark, well not unless it's night time. It's because it always faces away from Earth. Dark as in unknown. Like the dark continent.'

'Or dark chocolate?' Amy said.

'Exactly… What?'

'Kidding,' she told him.

The astronaut led them to a doorway. It was thick metal with a locking wheel on the outside. A red light glowed above the wheel.

Through a small window set in the door, Amy could see the other astronauts carrying the stretcher through a similar door, which they closed behind them. The glass was so thick that the image was distorted.

A green light replaced the red one above the locking wheel, and the astronaut spun it, then pulled the heavy door open. As he turned to allow Amy and the Doctor inside, Amy saw his shoulder had a US flag emblazoned on it. Beneath that was printed REEVE.

Inside the sealed airlock, there was a hiss as the small room pressurised. As soon as they were through the inner door, the astronaut reached up and twisted his helmet, then lifted it from his head. Beneath it he was wearing a white balaclava, which he also tugged off, revealing short, black hair. His face was rugged, but handsome and his eyes were as grey as surface of the moon.

The Doctor helped Amy remove her helmet before taking off his own. The astronaut's eyes widened as Amy's red hair cascaded out over her shoulders. She laughed. 'Don't you have girls in space?'

The astronaut smiled. 'We got a few. I'm Reeve, by the way. Captain Jim Reeve.'

He put his helmet on a shelf next to a dozen other identical helmets. They were in a large locker room, with shelves and cupboards where the spacesuits and equipment were stored. The Doctor was already struggling out of his suit. He still wore his jacket – slightly crumpled – underneath.

'Neat suits,' Reeve commented. 'They must be quite new.'

'Newer than you think,' the Doctor said, glancing at Amy.

'No idents, I notice.' Reeve tapped the name badge on his shoulder. 'I'll need to see some ID before I break the news to Colonel Devenish that we've got company.'

'I'd have thought he'd be glad of some help,' Amy said.

'You'd think that, yeah.' From his tone, it was an expectation that was probably not going to be fulfilled.

'Well, I'm Amy – Amy Pond. And this is the Doctor.'

'And you're here to fix the quantum displacement?'

'Absolutely,' the Doctor agreed.

'Only, since it's failed big time – how exactly did you get here?'

'Oh, we have our own portable system,' the Doctor said. 'Keep it in a box.'

'A box?'

'The box is blue.'

'Yeah, we got a signal about that. Going to bring it into the base. So that's something else that's got smaller, then,' Reeve said. 'We keep our quantum displacement system in a whole module. Rooms of equipment. No idea what it does.'

'Oh the theory's easy enough,' the Doctor assured him. 'It's like quantum entanglement. Only different. Instead of tying atoms and molecules together so they exhibit the same behaviour, you tie whole different locations together so they become the same place.'

'Oh yeah, easy,' Amy said.

Reeve laughed. 'All I know is, I can walk from here along a predefined path and end up in the Texan desert outside Base Hibiscus, and the Hibiscus folks can walk through the desert to get to the moon. So long as it works, that's all I'm interested in.'

'Except, it doesn't work,' the Doctor said. 'And now people are dead.'

'Like that woman and her dog,' Amy added.

'Yes,' the Doctor said. 'Which all suggests a sudden failure, then the system corrected itself – so that the man in the park ended up back in the park. And now you say it's bust again.'

'Totally,' Reeve agreed.

'I don't suppose you have a lead?' the Doctor asked.

'None at all. Oh, Jackson and the scientists are working on it but...' Reeve's voice tailed off as he saw the Doctor's expression. It was a mixture of amusement and sympathy.

'For the dog,' the Doctor said. 'I mean, was the dog on a lead?'

Reeve blinked. 'I guess so. I don't know. Is it important?'

'No idea,' the Doctor admitted. 'But it would prove the woman and the dog are an item. As it were. Rather than random dog and accidental woman.'

'Oh we got ID through from Base Hibiscus, if that's what you mean.'

'So you know who she is?' Amy asked.

'And the dog?' the Doctor checked.

'Yeah. It's just you guys I'm not sure about,' Reeve told them. 'Have you got any ID before I go tell the Colonel that the cavalry's arrived?'

'Think we might have strayed in too?' Amy asked.

'It happens. Wildlife strays in occasionally. Not a lot of it from the desert, and the dispersal link is only open at scheduled times. Had an eagle fly right through the gateway once. Dropped dead, of course. I admit, accidents like that don't normally wear spacesuits. But you turn up out of nowhere claiming to know all about a secret US project and, with all due respect, you guys don't sound very American.'

The Doctor flipped open his wallet of psychic paper. 'We've come to help. Here you go,' he said, waving it under Reeve's nose. 'Our Access All Areas pass from Base Hibiscus. Allows us to go anywhere, see anything, talk to anyone.'

Captain Reeve nodded. 'It does that,' he agreed. 'Just one thing though – why is it printed back to front?'

The Doctor frowned. 'I told you that would never work,' he said to Amy. 'He ruined it, didn't I say so? Signed his name on it. Ruined it.' He stuffed the wallet back inside his jacket pocket.

Amy ignored him. 'It's a security thing,' she told Reeve. 'Makes it harder to forge. So, can we see Colonel Devenish now, please?'

Chapter

4

Colonel Cliff Devenish was giving a briefing when Captain Reeve brought in the new arrivals. To say it was disruptive would be an understatement.

'So, let me get this straight,' Devenish was saying to Professor Jackson. 'You have no idea what's gone wrong, or how to fix it. Or even if it *can* be fixed?'

At that moment, the door of the briefing room opened and Reeve walked in. Behind him came a young man with what looked like an out-of-control comb-over, except he wasn't going bald, and a young woman with fiery red hair wearing a skirt far shorter than regulation length. 'Sir,' Reeve started to explain as the twenty people in the room gaped.

'Oh hi, don't mind us,' the comb-over guy said. 'Just carry on. Pretend we're not here. We'll behave. We'll take our milk and sit at the back.'

'Quiet as a mouse,' the redhead said. 'Two mice, in fact.'

The man stood looking round, apparently perplexed. 'Spare seats?' he wondered. 'Two together for preference. We're a pair. I mean, there's two of us.'

'Friends,' the woman said. 'Colleagues. Um, sorry – are we interrupting?'

'We didn't *mean* to interrupt,' the man said. Somehow he was standing at the front of the briefing room next to Colonel Devenish. 'But can I just ask, any unusual activity through the quantum displacement recently? I mean, anything come through that shouldn't? Anything you've sent or received that was a first. Could be anything, a strange-looking moon rock, a hamburger, a flock of seagulls, a rickshaw, anything.'

'You thinking something might have thrown off the quantum lock?' Jackson asked.

'If it had the right resonance. Well, the wrong resonance actually. Quartz embedded in rock, hot onion in a hamburger, the atmospheric fluctuation caused by a multitude of birds' wings. And who knows what might be carried by a rickshaw. That would be at the other end, of course. Wouldn't get any atmospheric fluctuation up here, would you.' The man's mouth cracked open into a huge grin and he flicked his hair out of his eyes.

'Doctor...' the woman said gently. She'd found a seat in the front row. There was another empty chair beside her.

'Sorry, but I thought that was funny.'

'No, I mean, you're hijacking the meeting,' she explained. She patted the chair beside her.

'Right. Sorry. Carry on – don't mind us.'

The man went and sat down next to the woman. He stuck his legs out as far as they would go, and mimed zipping his mouth shut. He made some indistinct sounds, but didn't open his mouth. To the increasingly irritated Devenish, the muffled noises sounded like: 'In your own time.'

'It's all right,' the woman said in a stage whisper, seeing Devenish's darkening expression. She pointed to the man, then to herself. 'The cavalry's arrived.'

Amy wasn't really surprised that the meeting ended shortly after they arrived. She had no illusions about the effect the Doctor had on people, and she could well imagine how disconcerted Colonel Devenish was to find two strangers, each with a different British accent, gate-crashing his secret briefing about secret problems with secret equipment on his secret moonbase.

The Colonel seemed slightly mollified by Reeve's explanations, such as they were. Reeve was obviously Colonel Devenish's right-hand man – although he was outranked by Major Carlisle.

A handful of people stayed behind after the briefing meeting broke up. Reeve was one, and Major Andrea Carlisle was another. She was a severe-looking woman in her thirties, Amy guessed. Her blonde hair was cut above the collar, and her nose was thin and prominent, giving her a slightly haughty look. Her manner matched, and Amy could see why Devenish got on better with the more easy-going, slightly younger Captain Reeve.

'We should verify these people's authenticity with Base Hibiscus,' Major Carlisle said, her New York accent as clipped and sharp as her tone.

'I've checked their papers,' Reeve said. 'They're on the level, so far as I can tell. Hell, how could they be here if they weren't?'

'We've got a dead woman and stiff dog who shouldn't be here, but they are,' Carlisle pointed out.

'That's a good point, actually,' the Doctor called from where he was still sitting in the front row of seats. 'Though we did dress more formally, and sensibly, than the poor deceased.'

'And he knows more about quantum displacement than I'll ever understand,' Reeve added.

'Not hard,' Major Carlisle snapped.

'Children,' the Doctor admonished.

'Hey – you can talk,' Major Carlisle told him. 'You don't look old enough to hold a doctorate. What are you a doctor of, anyway? Wit and sarcasm?'

The Doctor frowned as if trying desperately to remember. 'Er, no. I don't think so. I did get a degree in rhetoric and oratory from the University of Ursa Beta, but that was purely honorary. I asked if I had to make an acceptance speech, but they said there was no need. Seemed to defeat the object really, so I never mention it…' He leaped to his feet and stared at Major Carlisle. 'But it doesn't matter, does it? All that matters is whether you want your quantum displacement system fixed. If not, then we'll be going.'

'And if we do?' Colonel Devenish prompted.

'We'll be staying. But I'll need to know all about this Base Diana. What it's for, how long it's been here, where the canteen is, everything.'

'You don't know?' Major Carlisle said with an ill-concealed sneer.

'Never needed to know, not till now,' Amy told her.

'And everything round here is need-to-know, right?' the Doctor added. 'So *now* we do need to know.'

'Professor Jackson?' Devenish said.

Amy had not noticed the other man in the room. He was still sitting in the back row of seats. Now he stood up. He was a thin, wiry man with close-cut grey hair and eyes to match.

'Well, I'm not proud. I'll take help from wherever I can get it. Professor Charles Jackson,' he introduced himself, walking briskly to the front of the room. 'I'm in charge of the scientific side of things here, so maybe I'm the best person to give you a tour and explain the set-up. I'm also the only one here who has any idea how the quantum displacement system is supposed to work.' He paused. 'And my knowledge is patchy at best.'

Jackson seemed happy to show the Doctor and Amy round the base. He was friendly and helpful. 'Sorry about the military,' he said as soon as he was alone with the Doctor and Amy. 'They like everything regimented and ordered, not surprisingly. If it doesn't fit into one of their boxes, they get rather worked up about it.'

'Whereas you have a more open mind?' the Doctor said.

'I'm a scientist. New and strange ideas are my business. Same as you, I guess?'

The Doctor nodded. 'I'm a scientist. Amongst other things. And Amy certainly has an open mind.'

'You must have,' Jackson said to Amy, 'if you accept quantum displacement.'

'I've seen weirder things,' Amy told him.

Jackson raised an eyebrow, but didn't ask what she meant. 'How about I give you a quick tour of Base Diana? Then we can go to my office and talk about how you intend to proceed.'

'Sounds good to me,' the Doctor agreed. 'Sound good to you?' he asked Amy.

'Delightful.'

Just as it looked from the outside, the base was constructed from large modules connected by rectangular corridors. What could not be seen from outside was that the base also extended downwards, into more of the modules buried in the ground. Most of the base was taken up with living accommodation for the dozen soldiers, their three officers – Reeve, Carlisle and Devenish – and the few scientists that worked for Jackson. The majority of what was left was storage. Huge metal tanks held oxygen and hydrogen. Dried food was kept in large plastic drums and cartons. There was a canteen and a large kitchen, where the soldiers took it in turns to play chef.

'Someone had the foresight to keep you well stocked with food and water and oxygen,' the Doctor remarked. 'Rather than just relying on the quantum link for supplies.'

'I think it's habit,' Jackson confessed. 'Base Diana was first set up in the mid 1970s. The quantum displacement link was just a theory then, so they relied on moonshots to deliver supplies, though we have ready access to water. No one knew how long they could carry on before someone found out and called a halt.'

'Found out?' Amy said. 'But everyone knew didn't they? I mean, I know about Apollo 11 and Neil Armstrong. One small step for man and all that.'

'I'm guessing there's stuff the public didn't know,' the Doctor said.

'Hell, there's stuff the *President* doesn't know! Officially, the moon missions stopped with Apollo 17. Too expensive, everyone said. Shows how much they know.'

'You mean it wasn't expensive?' Amy asked.

'Oh, it sure was.' Jackson paused to open a bulkhead door – typing a number into a keypad alongside it. 'But for every dollar spent on Apollo, the US earned *fourteen* dollars back from the technology, from related exports, from patents and expertise. Pretty good investment, really. But people forget that.'

'So it all stopped.'

'Officially,' Jackson said, gesturing for the Doctor and Amy to go through the door.

They found themselves in a large, narrow, curving room. One side was almost entirely taken up with a huge window that looked into the inside of the curve. It was broken by more of the bulkhead doors, stretching out of sight. Beside each was a numeric keypad. Outside the window a low, narrow corridor extended from each door to a central, circular hub. It was strange to see the elegant curves of the inner building after the straight lines that formed the entire construction of the rest of the base.

'And unofficially?' the Doctor was prompting.

'Unofficially, here we are. Base Diana. Apollo 18 brought the first module. Flat-packed, tiny, weighed almost nothing. A breeze would have blown it away, so we're lucky there's no atmosphere.'

'How many unofficial Apollo missions were there?' Amy asked.

'The last was Apollo 22, in June 1980. It brought the final components for the quantum displacement link. After that, we could just walk from Diana across the lunar surface, and into the Texan desert close to Base Hibiscus. And all this – the current base – came back the same way.'

'Just sent it in on trucks?' Amy said, amazed.

'Something like that.'

Amy nodded at the huge expanse of thick glass. 'And is that your laboratory? Where you do research into whatever it is you do research into?'

'I do research into the human mind,' Jackson said. 'Into what makes one man good and another bad. What makes someone so fanatical they can maim and kill without troubling their conscience.'

That wasn't what Amy had expected. 'And you do it in there?'

'No,' the Doctor said quietly. 'That's another storage facility, isn't it?'

His expression had darkened as Jackson was

speaking. Now he was staring at the man, his eyes hard as flint.

'That's right, Doctor,' Jackson said, not seeming to notice the change in the Doctor's demeanour. 'That's where we keep the prisoners.'

Chapter
5

'**You knew, didn't you**,' Amy accused the Doctor as they followed Jackson through the long, narrow room.

'I guessed, but only when I saw this room. There'll be a whole penal colony here in a few hundred years, not just a dozen cells in an isolated block down vacuum corridors.'

'I suppose you know 'cause you were locked up in it?'

He grinned. 'Pretty cool, huh?'

Professor Jackson's office was a contrast to the neat military efficiency of the rest of Base Diana. His moulded plastic desk was piled high with papers and journals. An in-tray overflowed onto a nearby chair. Shelves strained to hold their contents.

The clearest shelf was occupied by a large, upright, steel cylinder with a tap at the bottom. There was a black plastic lid on the top, and the Doctor prised it open and peered inside. Steam drifted out past his nose as he sniffed at the contents.

'Earl Grey?'

'That's right. My tea urn. My one vice.' Jackson smiled. 'That and a passion for tidiness, as you see,' he joked. 'Let me get you a cup.'

'Thank you. No milk.'

'Quite right. I don't have any milk.' Jackson turned to Amy. 'And for you?'

'No thanks.' Amy wasn't sure she fancied tea without milk. Even Earl Grey.

'Find yourselves seats. I'll only be a moment. Just move anything that's in the way. Once we've had some tea, I'll show you the quantum displacement equipment and with a bit of luck you can fix it and be on your way.'

Jackson busied himself at the tea urn, while the Doctor and Amy liberated two upright chairs from their contents. Jackson's desk was almost the full width of the room. Behind it a large window gave out across the desolate lunar surface.

'Nice view,' the Doctor said. 'So, tell us about the prisoners.'

'We have eleven at the moment, in the cells you saw.' Jackson sat at his desk, blowing on his tea to cool it. 'The corridors from the reception area to the prison hub are kept airless unless we need to get to a cell, or to have a prisoner come to us. They're kept in solitary confinement, obviously, but they have everything they need.'

'Everything except freedom and company then,' Amy pointed out.

'They're well looked after. They get food sent

over from the canteen, just like we eat. If we need to evacuate, the cells open automatically and the access tunnels are oxygenated. If a prisoner gets ill, we take them to the medical section.'

'Haven't seen that yet,' the Doctor said.

Jackson shrugged. 'Not much to see.'

'So why are they here, the prisoners?' Amy asked. 'I mean, what did they do?'

'I don't ask too many questions.'

'That's handy, especially for a scientist,' the Doctor murmured. 'Nice tea, by the way.'

'They're all recidivists,' Jackson went on. 'All criminals that have resisted any conventional attempts to rehabilitate them. Re-offenders. But most of them are here because of what they know, what they learned from their crimes – from hacking government systems, or stealing sensitive information and documents. That makes them too dangerous to set free, or to keep in the standard prison system back in the States. Most of them can't even see that their behaviour was *wrong*. No moral judgement or ethical awareness whatsoever.'

'That's ironic. So, you just keep them locked up here?' the Doctor said. He sipped his tea. 'How moral and ethical is that?'

Jackson set down his tea on one of the few empty spaces on his desk. 'They're here for their own good.'

'I've heard that before,' Amy retorted.

'No, I mean it. They're here for treatment.'

There was silence for a moment. Then the Doctor said: 'I thought you told us they were beyond help.'

'Beyond *conventional* help, yes.'

'Ah!' The Doctor leaped to his feet. Tea slopped over the edge of his cup, but he seemed not to notice. 'Your research – you're *experimenting* on them, right?'

'Yes,' Jackson said, apparently relieved the Doctor had worked this out. But then he saw the Doctor's face darken. 'No,' he corrected himself. 'Not experimenting as such. We have a process. It works. But we...' His voice tailed off.

'You're experimenting on the prisoners,' Amy said. 'Aren't you?'

'Well, I guess so. But it isn't like you think.'

'Tell us what we think,' the Doctor said.

'It isn't scalpels and brain surgery. It isn't *dangerous*. It won't harm them.'

The Doctor nodded. 'So you do it up here on the dark side of the moon for convenience, then. Not because what you're up to is dangerous or illegal or would offend the sensibilities of any decent human being on the planet where you daren't use this *process* of yours.'

'I thought you had an open mind,' Jackson snapped. 'But you're jumping to conclusions without knowing anything about our work here.'

'I know...' the Doctor said slowly, 'I know that you believe what you are doing is for the best. I don't doubt your motives for a moment.'

'Thank you.'

'But that doesn't mean we have to agree with it.'

'Then perhaps we must agree to differ.'

Amy watched the Doctor as his expression relaxed from grim determination into a boyish grin. 'Yeah, maybe,' he agreed. Then he drained the rest of his tea in a single gulp. 'First things first, though. Where's this quantum displacement equipment of yours?'

The Doctor was in his element. Amy was bored.

Professor Jackson had led them down an incongruously old-fashioned metal stairway to a level deep below the main base. The corridors down here were formed not from walls but from pipes and cables. The idea that people might have to navigate through them seemed to have been very much a secondary consideration.

'So where's the quantum stuff?' Amy asked as they walked past pipes that leaked jets of steam and tubes that dripped oil.

'It's here,' Jackson said simply. 'All of this.' He gestured around them.

'Could be better maintained,' the Doctor said, running his finger along an especially oily plastic tube and showing them the resulting stain. 'But the design is basically sound.'

'But we can fix it, right?' Amy asked.

The Doctor winked. 'We can fix anything.'

Ahead of them, through the maze of cables and wires, tubes and pipes, Amy saw something move. Just a glimpse of grey overall.

'Are there many technicians working down here?'

Jackson shook his head. 'No one comes down here.'

'I thought I saw someone.'

'Only us,' Jackson insisted.

'Amy's right,' the Doctor said. 'Someone else is down here. Wearing size seven boots.'

'You can tell the size of their shoes just from a glimpse of someone through the pipes and stuff?' Amy was impressed.

'Probably,' the Doctor said. 'You can estimate from their height, weight, speed. But it's much easier if you just look at the print they've left in the spilt oil.' He pointed down at the ground – at the smudged, oily black boot print close by.

'OK,' Amy decided. 'Less impressive.'

'It's Major Carlisle,' the Doctor said.

'That's more like it. You checked out her boots and can recognise the distinctive pattern of the sole?'

It was Jackson who punctured the illusion this time. 'No, she's standing right behind you.'

Amy almost yelped with surprise. But she managed to keep it bottled in. 'Didn't hear you sneaking round from the other side,' she said.

Carlisle frowned, but ignored her. 'It's time for the process run on Nine,' she said to Jackson.

'I thought we'd postpone, under the circumstances,' Jackson said, glancing uneasily at the Doctor.

'Don't mind me,' the Doctor said. 'I'd love a chance to watch you at work.'

'The circumstances have nothing to do with the process,' Carlisle said. 'Colonel Devenish is happy for you to go ahead. He knows you like to stick rigidly to your schedule.'

'By "happy", I assume you mean "insisting",' Jackson said. 'Very well.' He checked his watch. 'We still have a little time.'

'You'll have to set up yourself, remember,' Carlisle said.

'Shortage of staff?' the Doctor asked.

'Professor Jackson's assistant is... unavailable,' Carlisle said.

From the way Jackson shifted uneasily again at her words, Amy guessed this was information he had not been about to volunteer himself.

'We can help,' she offered brightly. 'We're good at setting things up.'

'And knocking them down again,' the Doctor added. 'In fact, there's no end to our talents.'

Major Carlisle regarded them both impassively. 'Imagine that,' she said.

Prisoner Nine was a tall, thin man. He didn't look to Amy like a hardened and uncontrollable criminal. He was brought into the Process Chamber by two armed soldiers. The man's head was bowed, revealing a bald patch in his dark brown hair. The overall effect was to make him look rather like a monk wearing plain grey overalls.

The Process Chamber itself was a small room rather like a surgical theatre. Instead of an operating table there was an angled chair like a dentist might use. On the wall facing the chair was what looked a bit like a CCTV camera pointing at the subject as he sat down.

The man's dark brown eyes were as weary as his general demeanour, and Amy sensed that he had been here before, knew what to expect, and was resigned to it.

For a moment, the man's eyes fixed on Amy. There was a frown of interest, or possibly suspicion. Then he quickly looked away again, as if embarrassed.

'You know the routine,' one of the soldiers said to the man. 'So no trouble this time, right?'

The man grunted what might have been an agreement or a threat. But he didn't resist as the other soldier strapped his wrists to the arms of the chair, then fastened a belt tightly across his waist. Finally, straps across the ankles ensured the man could hardly move.

The Doctor was watching Professor Jackson as the scientist busied himself at a control panel behind the operating chair. Jackson turned and glared at the Doctor at one point when he leaned right over his shoulder. Otherwise he seemed to ignore the extra attention.

'So what happens now?' Amy asked as Jackson straightened up.

'We operate the process from the observation room,' Jackson said. 'Like X-rays, brief exposure is harmless enough so the subject is in no danger. But we don't like to prolong exposure more than we have to.'

Something else that was like the dentist, Amy thought. It always worried her that when she had a routine X-ray of her teeth the dentist and nurse disappeared out of the door.

The observation room was behind the wall in front of the chair. The wall itself was actually a window, though it looked just like another wall from the prisoner's point of view.

The device that ended in the camera-like projection from the wall extended back through the observation room like a large articulated metal arm. There were controls set into the side of it, and Jackson adjusted several of these.

'I think we are ready,' he decided at last. The prisoner – Nine – stared back at him. Amy was sure he knew they were there, watching.

'What happens now?' Amy asked. 'How's this thing work?'

'It is rather complicated, and difficult to explain in a few words,' Jackson told her dismissively. Obviously he wasn't willing to share.

'Doctor?' Amy asked.

'Oh it's simple enough, from what I can see.' The Doctor ignored Jackson's irritated glare, and went on: 'Looks to me like it bombards areas of the brain with adapted alpha waves in an attempt to overwhelm the neural pathways and neutralise the electro-activity.'

'Brainwashing,' Amy said, hoping that this vague, blanket term was in some way applicable.

'Exactly,' the Doctor said.

'You've been reading my classified research reports,' Jackson accused.

The Doctor's excitement immediately grew. 'Really – you mean I'm right? That's terrific. It was just an educated guess. But hang on...' He tapped his chin with his finger. 'That means...' His eyes narrowed. 'You're not actually treating the patient at all, you're not correcting the impulses in their brains. You're removing them. Wiping them. Like Amy says – washing them away.'

'Only the bad, negative inclinations. The Keller-impulses.'

The Doctor's tone was quiet and dark. 'And who gave you the right to decide which ones are bad and which ones are normal?' he demanded.

Jackson was saved from having to answer as the door opened and Major Carlisle came in. With her was another woman, wearing a simple nurse's uniform. She looked about Amy's age, with mouse-brown hair cut into a bob and a scattering of freckles across her nose.

'This is Nurse Phillips,' Jackson said quickly, keen to change the subject. 'We have to have a medic on hand whenever we process a prisoner. And now,' he went on, 'we are already behind schedule, so allow me to begin.'

'Begin what, exactly?' Amy asked.

'Despite the Doctor's reservations, this is a very minor procedure. We target a single memory strand – the memory of the trigger that sent our subject off the rails. That was identified in a previous session, and we are now going to remove that memory.'

'And replace it with what?' the Doctor asked.

'With nothing. We leave it blank. Wash it out, as you so eloquently put it.'

'The brain's like nature. Abhors a vacuum,' the Doctor said quietly. The hum of the machine became louder, and it seemed that only Amy had heard.

'You mean, they have to put another memory in to replace the old one?' she asked the Doctor, talking loudly above the building noise.

He nodded. 'Yes, otherwise the pattern will simply return, like remembering a dream a few hours later.'

'So their experiment will fail,' Amy said.

Her words were almost drowned out by the noise.

Not the sound of the machine as the power built and increased. The sound of the screams from the prisoner strapped to the chair in the next room.

Jackson turned from the controls, his face an expression of sudden surprise and fear.

Nurse Phillips' hand went to her mouth. Major Carlisle was already pulling open the door.

The Doctor pushed past and was out of the room before her, Amy close behind.

'Cut the power,' the Doctor yelled as he raced into the Process Chamber. 'Cut it now!'

Chapter
6

Although she was only moments behind him, the Doctor had already unstrapped the prisoner when Amy reached the Process Chamber. The hum of the equipment had died away.

The Doctor was listening to the man's chest. He straightened up and gently peeled back a closed eyelid.

'Just unconscious, I think,' the Doctor decided. 'Let's hope there's no permanent damage.'

'What went wrong?' Amy asked.

'Goodness knows. Could be anything. The tiniest mistake when you're messing with people's minds can be fatal. Power spike, power dip, power fluctuation.'

'Could be something to do with the power, then?'

The Doctor nodded. 'Or not.'

'Can he be moved?' Major Carlisle demanded.

'Moved where?' Amy asked.

'Back to his cell. This man is a dangerous criminal.'

'Oh you're all heart, aren't you,' the Doctor told her.

'Can he be moved?' Carlisle repeated, but this time she asked Nurse Phillips who was watching them from the doorway.

'I don't know. I expect so.' She sounded nervous. Amy guessed the process had not gone wrong before – at least, not like this.

The prisoner's eyelids were fluttering. The Doctor leaned over him.

'Are you all right?' he asked. 'Can you hear me?'

The man's breathing became ragged as he struggled to speak. His hands bunched into claws, which then tightened into fists. His back arched and his eyes snapped fully open as he screamed again.

The Doctor grabbed the man's shoulders, trying to hold him down. Amy hurried to help. The whole body was convulsing, the man's teeth clenched, sweat breaking out on his forehead.

'Not good,' the Doctor muttered. 'This is *so* not good.'

'Sedative,' Major Carlisle snapped. Nurse Phillips hurried to a drawer.

'Too late for that,' the Doctor told them. 'I'm really sorry about all this,' he murmured to the man.

For a moment, the man's vision seemed to clear. The convulsions became less extreme. He stared up at the Doctor, and Amy heard him clearly say:

'Doctor – is that you?'

The Doctor looked across at Amy. 'Who told him my name?'

Amy shook her head. 'How could he know you?'

'Doctor – help me,' the man gasped.

His voice was barely more than a whisper. Major Carlisle didn't seem to have heard. Jackson watched from the doorway. Nurse Phillips flicked a syringe full of clear liquid with her finger to release any air bubbles.

The prisoner's hand grabbed the Doctor's. 'Help me – they're here!'

'Who are? What are you talking about?' the Doctor whispered back urgently. 'What's the last thing you remember?'

'Remember?' The man frowned, in an effort to concentrate. 'Everything's so muzzy, lately. Since they came. But before that I was in here. I was setting the equipment for the first tests.'

'The equipment?' Amy looked at the Doctor, then back at the prisoner. 'Why would they let a prisoner set up the equipment'

'I'm not a prisoner,' the man said. His voice was fading. He slumped back in the chair. 'I built this. I set all this up. You have to believe me. I'm—'

Then the syringe stabbed into his upper arm and his voice choked off. The man's eyes closed. A great shiver ran through his body. Then he was still.

Nurse Phillips pulled out the syringe and stepped back.

'Oh thanks,' the Doctor said. 'That was a big help.'

'The man was distressed, in convulsions,' Nurse Phillips said. 'He needed sedating. Normally—'

'Normally?' the Doctor gave a mirthless laugh. 'What exactly is *normal* about this? About any of this?'

He shook his head sadly, like a frustrated parent giving up trying to explain something simple to an unhelpful child.

'Can we move him now?' Major Carlisle asked.

'You can do what you like with him,' the Doctor said, striding from the room. 'He's dead.'

Amy found the Doctor sitting at a table in the small canteen. He was the only person there, leaning back in his chair with his feet up on the table. His fingers were laced together behind his head as he stared at the ceiling.

'Did the nurse kill him?' Amy asked.

'Not on purpose.' The Doctor swung his legs off the table and jolted upright in the chair. 'No, that's not fair. It wasn't her fault at all. The sedative was just the last straw. He'd probably have died anyway.'

'And how come he knew you?'

'Been thinking about that.'

'And?'

'Remember I said the memory they were erasing had to be replaced with something?'

Amy nodded. 'Otherwise it just sort of reappears like the memory of a dream popping up later.'

'Maybe it wasn't intentional, but I think that man got someone else's memory. Or a bit of it.'

'So what did he mean by "They're here" and all that stuff?'

'Don't know. Maybe nothing. He was confused – well, he was dying, let's face it. Perhaps he meant the new memories in his head, who can tell? But something went wrong with Jackson's process.' The

Doctor's eyes flicked to the side as he looked past Amy. 'Talk of the devil.'

Amy turned and saw that the Professor had come into the canteen. He looked tired and worried.

'There was a power surge,' Jackson said, joining them at the table. He stared down at the plastic surface. 'Never happened before. And now the man's dead. I didn't even know his name – he was just Prisoner Nine.' He looked up at Amy and the Doctor, and Amy saw that his grey eyes had a haunted look to them. 'It must be connected to the same problem as the quantum displacement systems.'

'Possibly,' the Doctor agreed. 'I'd need to look at the receptors out on the lunar surface to be sure. Once I've checked the calibration of the equipment in the basement level, that is.'

'Can you really fix it?'

'If I want to,' the Doctor said.

Jackson was confused. 'Why might you not want to?'

The Doctor met the man's gaze. For several moments he said nothing. Then, when he did reply his voice was level and almost devoid of emotion. Amy could tell he was holding back his real feelings, but there was no mistaking what they were.

'I've seen enough of your process to know what your ultimate goal must be, Professor Jackson. Oh you make a good case for rehabilitating the prisoners, for erasing selected memories – maybe even replacing them. But that isn't what you're really aiming for, is it? You want to wipe the mind completely clean, create a blank template. And then overwrite it with a new personality. Am I right, or…' The Doctor leaned back in his chair and sniffed. 'Well, there's no *or* is there, because I am right.'

Jackson looked like he'd been thumped. But he recovered quickly. 'You're a very perceptive man, Doctor. But I don't understand your concern.'

'Concern?' the Doctor countered. '*Concern?*'

Jackson held his hand up. 'I offer the chance to swap the mind – the *life* – of a worthless criminal for someone who would otherwise be taken from us. Imagine it, the opportunity for a great musician or thinker, who is terminally ill, or just very old, to live on. To renew themselves, literally to have a new life in a new form. To become someone new, but with all that brilliance preserved.'

Put like that, Amy didn't think it sounded so bad. Except that someone else had to lose their mind.

'It's not all it's cracked up to be,' the Doctor said quietly. 'A great musician who finds his new body is tone deaf? A thinker whose thoughts inhabit the mind of a simpleton?'

'But it wouldn't be random. You'd get to choose, to fit the mind to a suitable donor. No problem.'

Amy knew what the Doctor was really so opposed to. 'The donor has to die,' she said. '*That's* the problem.'

'As I said before, perhaps we should agree to differ, until the systems are fixed. My process is far from that stage, and under the current circumstances I shan't be doing any more tests.'

The Doctor nodded thoughtfully. 'I'll fix your systems. After that, we'll talk again.'

'Fair enough. I look forward to it.' Jackson stood up. 'I suppose we have rather overlooked the ethics of what we're doing while we've been caught up in the excitement of actually doing it.'

Amy waited until Jackson had gone before she asked: 'Can you really fix their quantum thingie systems?'

'Oh, probably.' The Doctor leaped to his feet. He jumped up and down a couple of times. 'I'd have thought a power surge would affect the artificial gravity, but it's fine. That's lucky.'

'Unless Jackson's lying about the power surge,' Amy pointed out.

'Not sure why he should. Why don't you go and see Nurse Phillips?'

'See if he's lying about whether there have been any other accidents, you mean?'

'Exactly,' the Doctor said. 'Jackson said she was there for every process session. She's young enough to be a bit chatty, a bit indiscreet.'

'A bit intimidated?'

'If need be.' The Doctor grinned. 'Don't frighten her too much, scary lady.'

Amy's eyes widened. 'As if.'

There was only one patient in the base sickbay. Nurse Phillips was checking the equipment that monitored the sleeping woman's vital signs. Amy had little idea what any of the blips and traces and numbers actually meant.

'What's wrong with her?' she asked.

If the young nurse was surprised to see her, she

didn't show it. Her pale grey eyes flicked back to the woman in the bed. 'I wish I knew.'

'Who is she?'

'Liz Didbrook. She is, or was, Professor Jackson's assistant.'

Amy looked at the sleeping woman. She was restless. Her head twisted on the pillow and she murmured quietly to herself. She looked to be in her early thirties. Her dark hair was damp with sweat.

'Does she have a fever? Is she infectious?'

The woman's eyes flickered open as Amy spoke.

'Neither,' said Nurse Phillips. 'It's some sort of nervous breakdown. Brought on by stress, Professor Jackson thinks. We keep her sedated.'

Not as sedated as Prisoner Nine, Amy hoped. She leaned over the bed, listening. 'What is she saying?'

'Just nonsense,' Nurse Phillips said. 'We'd get her to a hospital in Texas, only...'

'Only there's no way home right now,' Amy finished.

'It's just gibberish,' Nurse Phillips said as Amy continued to listen.

The woman – Liz – was staring at Amy, her expression suddenly alert. 'You're new.'

'Yes. I'm Amy. I'm here to help.'

'Giant turtles live for ages,' Liz said. 'Evolution is all about survival of the fittest.'

'You see – nonsense,' Nurse Phillips said. She turned and walked out of the room.

'But fittest doesn't mean strongest,' Liz went on. 'It means most apt. That's why they want us.'

'Why who wants us?' Amy said.

'The white rabbit is running late,' Liz said. 'X marks the spot where the treasure is buried. When the sky is dark, the wolves are running.'

'She's right,' Amy said quietly. 'Just gibberish. Hey – get well soon.' She patted the woman gently on the shoulder. 'I'll see you, yeah?'

'Don't go! They're here.' Liz struggled to sit up. 'I have to… Trains are delayed on all routes. Even Route 66. Distraction. They're delayed by the distraction.'

'The trains?' Amy frowned. There was something in what she said – something close to making sense, but clouded in the rest of it. Distraction. 'Are you saying that you have to distract them. Whoever *they* are?' She looked round. 'Can they hear us? Are they listening?'

'Listen from the inside – it's so much clearer. So much clearer inside the mind. Distractions abound. Distractions are good. Good, bad and ugly. Spaghetti Westerns for tea and lunch and dinner and breakfast and making a meal of it.'

Liz's hand shot out from under the sheets and grabbed Amy's wrist. 'I can't tell you if they're here. Flies in the ointment. Rain in the wind. Spanners in the works. Wolves in the wood.'

The woman's eyes were a startling blue as she gazed intently at Amy. 'What are you telling me?' Amy asked. 'You mean the systems here? Spanners in the works – is that what you mean?'

'Spanners in the works,' Liz said. Her grip on Amy's wrist tightened urgently. 'Gremlins in the process.'

'The process?' Amy repeated. There was a sound

behind her and she turned, pulling her arm away from Liz's grip.

'She really should rest,' Nurse Phillips said. How long had she been there, watching? 'It's just nonsense, all of it. Pay no attention.'

Amy looked back at Liz – now slumped down in the bed. The colour seemed to have drained from her eyes, so the blue was almost grey.

'The grey African elephant is the largest mouse in the western hemisphere and comes in nine different shades of pink,' Liz murmured. 'Remember what I said.' Her eyes slowly closed, and her words became just mumbles.

'I'll remember,' Amy said quietly. Louder, to Nurse Phillips, she said: 'You're right. She's obviously flipped out. She's just talking rubbish.'

Chapter

7

The damaged area was easy to spot once the Doctor knew where to look.

It took him a while to work out the design of the quantum displacement systems. But once he'd got the hang of it, he could trace through the various components. He already had a good idea where the problem must be.

'Accidental?' Major Carlisle asked.

A whole section of pipes and tubes had been blown out. Cables hung loose and a junction box was a blackened mess.

'Difficult to tell,' the Doctor admitted. He licked his thumb and forefinger and then griped the end of a wire. It sparked violently. 'Well, that's something.'

Major Carlisle winced as the Doctor inspected his blackened fingers. 'But it could be sabotage?'

'Could be. You expecting sabotage?'

She didn't answer.

'The good news is that it shouldn't take long to fix. Just reconnect all the bits and bobs, and bypass this junction box.'

'Bits and bobs?'

'Then realign the receptors outside and bits and bobs your uncle.'

'You're either very brilliant or completely mad,' Major Carlisle told him.

'Both, actually. But veering towards the brilliant. You don't want to see me when I'm mad.' The Doctor already had his sonic screwdriver out and was reattaching wires. 'You going to stand there watching me?'

'What do you want me to do?'

'Go away. No, I don't mean it like that,' he went on quickly. 'Just don't want to be distracted at a crucial moment. Can you tell Colonel Devenish that everything's under control, and that I'll need to go out on the surface and test things and realign the receptors.'

It seemed only a few moments later that a shadow fell across the Doctor as he finished the final few connections. But he realised that almost an hour had passed.

Captain Reeve waited until the Doctor was done before he spoke. 'The Colonel says it's fine for you to go out on the surface. You can have permission, no problem.'

'I didn't ask for permission.'

'Yeah, he knows. But he's given it anyway. That way he can put conditions on it.'

'Conditions?' The Doctor closed up the blackened

shell of the now empty junction box.

'Well, just the one. He's going out there with you.'

Captain Reeve helped the Doctor and Colonel Devenish suit up. Soon the two of them were walking out across the surface of the moon. Devenish's bulky white spacesuit was a contrast to the Doctor's more advanced and streamlined red one.

'We're on a closed communications circuit,' Devenish said. 'No one else can hear us.'

'And why are you telling me this?' the Doctor wondered.

'Just thought I'd mention it. Same as Major Carlisle just happened to mention to me that the damage to the systems could be sabotage.'

'*Could* be. Or it could be accidental. An overloaded component, a power surge. Whatever. I'll have a better idea when I check the receptors. If they've mis-phased then it could be just bad luck. But if the target location has actually been reset, that suggests it's deliberate.'

They walked on in silence for several minutes.

'I don't think Major Carlisle likes me very much,' the Doctor said eventually.

Devenish's bark of laughter echoed inside his helmet. 'I don't think Major Carlisle likes anyone very much. Her daddy was a general,' he went on. 'She's got a lot to live up to.'

'She doesn't have to live up to anything.'

'True, but she thinks she does. Then again, my daddy had a gas station in Colorado and died of boredom before he was 60, so what do I know?'

'Maybe you have even more to live up to,' the Doctor told him.

The receptors were like metal mushrooms poking up through the dry dusty grey of the landscape. There were two lines, stretching to the foreshortened horizon.

'We only need to recalibrate one each side,' the Doctor explained. 'I can set them to pass the new settings on down the line.'

'You know where you're setting it for?'

'Not a clue. But there should be a hardware reset that keys it back to the original location. Base Hibiscus, you called it?'

'Deep in the heart of Texas,' Devenish said. The Doctor could hear the smile in his voice.

Amy passed several soldiers as she made her way through the base, but no one questioned who she was or what she was doing. And Nurse Phillips seemed to have no idea that she was being followed.

Maybe she'd got it wrong, thought Amy, keeping her distance and hoping the young nurse wouldn't turn round and see her. Maybe Nurse Phillips was as honest as they come. But she'd given the prisoner the injection that killed him. She'd overheard the nonsense – and maybe not so non-sense – that Liz Didbrook had spoken to Amy. She'd been present at every processing and assured Amy she'd never before witnessed any problems at all... Come on – no problems at all, ever, in a series of experiments to wipe people's minds and replace their thoughts and memories?

But maybe, just maybe, Amy was wasting her time and Nurse Phillips was as naive and straightforward and innocent as she seemed.

Or maybe not, Amy decided as she ducked into a doorway close to Jackson's office. Nurse Phillips glanced furtively over her shoulder before she knocked and went in.

The door was closed, so Amy had to press her ear hard against it to hear anything. She hoped no one came and caught her doing it. Might be kind of hard to explain.

'Carlisle,' Jackson's muffled voice said from the other side of the door.

'So soon?' Nurse Phillips replied.

'This Doctor worries me. Perhaps he really can repair the systems. Carlisle will know, she was with him. I've asked her to join us in the Process Chamber in a few minutes.'

Realising this must mean they were about to emerge from the office, Amy ran quickly back down the corridor. If she could get to the Process Chamber ahead of them she could find somewhere to hide and hear what Major Carlisle thought of the Doctor. Amy smiled to herself as she ran. Actually, she could probably guess that one right now.

Amy had forgotten how spartan the Process Chamber was. There was nowhere she had any chance of hiding. The Observation Room was just as unhelpful. So Amy's best option was to wait in one of the nearby storerooms, and listen at the door again.

She didn't have long to wait. Jackson and Nurse Phillips were only a couple of minutes behind her, and Major Carlisle joined them in the corridor mere moments later.

'This Doctor,' Jackson said without preamble. 'Can he really fix the quantum displacement systems?'

With the storeroom door open just a crack, Amy clearly heard Carlisle's response.

'I think he can. He seems young and flippant, but there's an underlying astuteness to him. It's hard to describe.'

'And the girl?' Nurse Phillips said. Amy stiffened.

'Not sure, to be honest. But again, I wouldn't underestimate her. Someone at Hibiscus obviously rates them both. Maybe even Walinski himself.'

'More likely that jumped-up technician Hecker,' Jackson said.

'Yes,' Carlisle said. 'Well, if that's all you wanted...?'

'There was one other thing,' Jackson said. 'In the Process Chamber. Something I'd like you to take a look at.'

'Is it important?'

'Oh yes.' Jackson's voice was suddenly low and slightly sinister. 'It's certainly important.'

Amy heard the door to the Process Chamber close behind them. When she stepped out of the storeroom, the corridor was empty.

If she had looked out just a few moments before, as Nurse Phillips followed Jackson and Carlisle into the Process Chamber, she would have been surprised to see the young nurse taking a syringe from her jacket pocket.

*

'Not as easy as I thought,' the Doctor confessed. 'Looks like we'll have to reset them all individually.'

He closed up the cover on the side of the stumpy receptor and moved on to the next one.

'I'll do the other side,' Colonel Devenish said.

'Sure you can manage?'

'I just watched you. Looked easy enough. I'm not a complete dork, you know.'

The Doctor grinned inside his helmet. 'Never thought you were.'

'I did wonder about you though,' Devenish said. 'But Jackson was willing to give you the time of day.'

'And you respect his judgement.'

'I used to. Now...' Devenish unclipped the inspection hatch on the side of the receptor. 'I'm not sure I trust him any more.'

'Dubious ethics,' the Doctor guessed, moving on to another of the receptors.

'Oh he's always had those. But recently... I don't know. It's nothing you can put your finger on. But he's *changed*.'

The Doctor closed up the cover and moved on down the line. 'Why are you telling me?'

'Because you're from off base. I don't know who you are, but I reckon I can trust you.'

'Suggesting you can't trust your own team,' the Doctor realised.

'Suggesting I don't know if I can trust them or not. There's something going on here on my base. Something I don't understand. Something I don't like.'

'Something to do with the people?'

'Or perhaps I'm just getting paranoid. But then this sabotage...'

'If it was sabotage.'

'You said you'd be able to tell, once you checked the receptors,' Devenish reminded him. 'So you tell me.'

The Doctor closed the cover of the receptor he'd just reset and stood up. He turned to find Devenish facing him, his face distorted through the thick visor of the helmet.

'Look.' The Doctor pointed along the path made by the two parallel lines of receptors. Instead of disappearing over the lunar horizon, the path now shimmered in the heat. The grey dust either side of the path was pale sand. A line of blue sky cut downwards from the black heavens.

'It worked!' Devenish said. 'Doctor – you're a genius.'

'Thanks. We'd better reset the rest of them. And, yes I am a genius,' the Doctor went on. 'Because you're not paranoid at all. It would take a genius to spot it, but what happened here was definitely sabotage.'

Amy hadn't even reached the door to the Process Chamber when she heard the noise. Something slammed back into the other side of the door. Shouting, grunts, something metal clattered to the floor.

'Hold her!' Jackson's voice shouted.

Amy didn't know if she should go in and help or stay where she was. But who needed help – what was going on?

In just a few moments, the noise died down. Amy

pressed her ear to the door. This was becoming a habit.

'She's tougher than she looks,' Jackson said. 'Which could be useful.'

Amy couldn't hear the reply – did he mean Major Carlisle or Nurse Phillips?

'I've programmed a Blank. One of the soldiers,' Jackson was saying now. 'If the Doctor manages to repair the systems, the Blank can simply disable them again. But in light of what Major Carlisle said, you had better send him in anyway.'

'I'm on it. The Doctor and Devenish went outside, to reset the receptors.' Nurse Phillips' voice was faint but audible now. She must be moving back towards the door.

'In the worst case, they'll be stuck back on Earth,' Jackson said. 'Worst for us, that is. It could be a lot worse for them.'

Amy backed slowly away. She didn't know what they meant by a 'Blank' but one thing was clear – the Doctor was in danger and she was the only one who could help him. But how?

The desert stretched as far as the eye could see in every direction. The Doctor and Colonel Devenish had reached the last of the receptors.

'It always amazes me,' Devenish said, watching the Doctor make the final adjustments, 'the way you can just walk off the moon into the desert. The whole notion that you can be in two places at once.'

'That's what quantum mechanics is all about,' the Doctor told him.

'I know that. At least, I know it intellectually. The reality of it, that's rather different.'

'I know what you mean. It's all well and good at the atomic level. But when its actually people and places... You know this is surprisingly sophisticated. I didn't think there was a direct link from Earth to the moon until T-Mat got going and that won't be for a while yet.' The Doctor stood up. 'There we are. All done. There's no charge.'

Devenish reached up and unclipped his helmet. He twisted it, and lifted it off his head, taking a deep breath of the warm, dry desert air.

'That is just so liberating,' he said.

The Doctor removed his own helmet. 'Gets hot in these things, doesn't it.'

'Here in the desert, but not on the moon.' Devenish bounced experimentally on his feet. 'Feel that Earth gravity. Every time I come back I decide I need to go on a diet.'

From her hiding place behind the storeroom door, Amy watched Nurse Phillips and Professor Jackson emerge from the Process Chamber. There was no sign of Major Carlisle. Jackson made his way to the observation room. Nurse Phillips hurried away down the corridor.

Amy waited until they were both out of sight. Decision time – should she try to see what Jackson was up to? Maybe find out what had happened to Major Carlisle?

Or should she follow Nurse Phillips? She must be going to check on the 'Blank', whatever that was. Something to do with disabling the quantum systems again. The systems the Doctor was trying to mend.

Stepping out from the storeroom, careful to make as little noise as possible, Amy ran down the corridor after Nurse Phillips.

The world was muzzy and unfocused. Andrea Carlisle blinked rapidly in an effort to clear her vision. Her head was full of buzzing. She tried to move her arm, and nothing happened.

Gradually she became aware that she was strapped down. Her wrists and ankles were restrained. There was a strap across her waist. Her head was held in position by a brace. She was half lying, half sitting on a padded chair, facing a bare wall.

Except it wasn't completely bare. There was something, if she could just focus on it. Something projecting from the wall, pointing right at her...

And suddenly she was completely awake, straining at the straps. She was in the Process Chamber. The buzzing wasn't inside her head, it was the hum of the equipment powering up. She remembered coming into the room with Jackson and Phillips – the sudden pain in her neck. A glimpse of the syringe being removed. Lashing out, shoving Nurse Phillips back against the door, knocking things over... Then darkness.

And now this.

The end of the probe was glowing. The hum rose in pitch and volume.

Jackson's voice was calm but clear through the speakers: 'I'm so glad you're awake, Major. Take a last look at your world before you surrender yourself to us.'

Her vision blurred again. All she could see was the glow of the probe. All she could hear was the rising hum of the machine.

And the brittle scuttling like the claws of a rat as *something* crept into her mind and began to eat her memories...

*

A figure stood in the shadows close to the bottom of the metal stairway down to the basement levels. Stock-still, the soldier might have been on guard duty – except that his eyes were closed. His face was relaxed and slack. His arms hung limply by his side, his shoulders slumped forwards.

Nurse Phillips watched him for a few moments, her mouth twisting into the trace of a smile.

'It is time,' she said softly.

The soldier's eyes snapped open. He straightened up, alert and ready.

'You know what to do,' Nurse Phillips told him.

She watched the soldier march stiffly away before returning to the stairs.

The metal treads echoed under her feet, masking the sound of lighter footsteps below. Amy glanced up at the disappearing figure before hurrying after the soldier.

Keeping well back, she followed the dark figure through the maze of pipework and cables, past control consoles and computer terminals. He seemed to know exactly where he was headed. Finally, the soldier stopped in front of a control panel mounted on the wall. He stared at it for several seconds, and Amy was tempted just to ask him what he was doing.

Then the soldier turned and picked up a length of metal pipe that was lying nearby. He weighed it in his hand, then smashed it down on the controls.

Sparks erupted from the console. The constant hum of the machinery changed in pitch, becoming laboured and uncertain.

Amy ran forward. 'Stop that – stop that now!'

The soldier seemed not to hear. Again and again he smashed the pipe down on the console. A whole section exploded. Smoke billowed out from a panel.

The soldier raised the pipe yet again. Amy grabbed his wrist, pulling hard to try to unbalance the man. He barely noticed, tearing his wrist free and slamming the pipe down once more.

Apparently satisfied, the soldier moved along. He dropped the pipe, which clattered to the floor and rolled away – bent and dented from its work. The soldier reached out, lacing his fingers through a mass of wires. And ripped them away. Sparks crackled round the broken ends. The lights dimmed for a moment, then came back up again. A klaxon began to sound. The surviving parts of the control console were lit up with red warning lights – flashing erratically.

'Right, that's enough.' Amy ran at the man. She lowered her shoulder, hammering into him from behind.

The soldier was slammed forwards into the wall. His body jolted and shimmered as he hit the broken ends of the live wires. The lights flickered again, then went out completely.

The last thing Amy saw before the darkness descended was the soldier turning towards her – his face blackened, eyes staring and unblinking. No expression. Blank.

The helmet was only inches away from him across the ground. But the Doctor was never going to reach it.

Colonel Devenish collapsed to his knees, his hands scrabbling at his throat as he tried to breathe.

The desert sand shimmered in the heat, blurring into the cold grey landscape of the moon.

The Doctor's own breaths were painful gasps now. His throat burned for lack of air. The cold was freezing his skin, drying his eyes, tightening across his whole body.

He tried to crawl towards Devenish. But the Colonel was as far away as the helmet – inches. Inches out of reach as the cold airless night closed in.

The scrabbling and scratching in Major Carlisle's head was unbearable. Everything else dissolved – senses, memories, thought itself. Boiled away as something clawed and tore its way through her mind.

She tried to focus on the voice – urgent, shouting, but filtered like it was through a loudspeaker somewhere.

'Nurse Phillips – the power's off. I'm at a critical stage. We need the power back. What's that Blank done? I need power now…'

Somehow she sensed that this was good. She could feel the claws falter, the scratching diminish. The world swam into focus – the Process Chamber, lit red by emergency battery lights. The probe, its light flickering and dying.

For the briefest moment, Carlisle's mind was free again. For a few precious seconds she was aware of the memories and thoughts that had been scratching their way into her mind. Then the probe flared back into life, dazzlingly bright, burning into her eyes.

Amy blinked as after a few unsettling moments

the lights came back on abruptly. The noise of the equipment seemed to stabilise, and she guessed a secondary generator or emergency system of some sort had cut in to take over from the damaged systems.

The soldier was still staring blankly at Amy, just as before the lights failed.

'What are you doing?' she demanded, bracing herself for the attack.

But the man didn't move. He just stood, staring. Unmoving. Then, slowly, his eyes closed. His shoulders slumped slightly – like he had fallen asleep while still on his feet.

As if he'd been switched off, Amy thought. Like a computer program that had reached the end, completed its task, and simply stopped.

On the lunar surface, a sudden, impossible breeze stirred the dust between the line of receptors. Two space helmets – one white, one red – lay half-buried. A gloved hand was stretched out towards one of the helmets in a final desperate dying attempt to reach it.

Then the breeze was gone, taking with it the last of the air. Leaving only the dust and the dead...

Chapter
9

A rasping breath wracked the Doctor's whole body. He wheezed and choked, coughing until his throat was raw. The ground beneath him was warm and sharp – like tiny knives cutting into his palms as he pressed down in an effort steady his body.

He was lying on his back, staring up at an azure sky. The faintest wisp of cloud skittered across his vision. The sun was a burning disc that hurt his eyes.

Slowly, as the coughing and gasping died away and he caught his breath, the Doctor pushed himself upwards. He sat staring round at the undulating landscape. Not the grey, barren moon, but the warm sandy desert. He climbed to his feet.

The lines of receptors had gone. The link was broken and they would be back on the moon. There was no sign either of the Doctor's helmet, or of Colonel Devenish. The Doctor sighed and shook his head sadly, knowing all too well what that must mean.

'Sabotage,' he murmured. The stiff desert breeze ruffled his hair and blew up a ground-hugging swirl of sand. 'Sabotage and murder.' He licked his finger and held it up, gauging the direction of the wind.

'Deep in the heart of Texas,' the Doctor remembered Devenish had said. Texas was enormous – the second largest US state. But he was sure someone had mentioned that Base Hibiscus was close to Houston. Assuming that the quantum link had actually brought them to Texas somewhere near the base. If not he could be anywhere. There was no guarantee, he thought ruefully, that this was even Earth.

Assuming the lines of receptors had been the start of a pathway to the base, and assuming too that he remembered which way they'd been aligned, the Doctor started walking through the empty desert.

'Could be worse,' he said to himself. 'It might have been Alaska.'

After a while, the Doctor was beginning to wish it was Alaska. Without the helmet, his spacesuit wasn't sealed and the heat got trapped inside. He stripped off the spacesuit and staggered on in his slacks and shirtsleeves, bow tie hanging untied round his neck. The breeze was cooling, but it whipped up the sand and blew it in his eyes so he could hardly see.

In the distance, peering through the bright sun and the stinging sand, the Doctor could see a dark cloud. More sand, swirling across the desert towards him. A sandstorm? He looked round, but there was nowhere to shelter – no cover whatsoever.

As the whirling sand grew closer, the Doctor saw that it was kicked up by a jeep, racing towards him through the desert. It slewed to a halt a few metres away, engine idling. Three uniformed soldiers jumped out of the back of the jeep and ran towards the Doctor, unshouldering their assault rifles.

The Doctor stood up and reached out to shake the nearest soldier's hand. The soldier took his hand, but dragged the Doctor forwards before spinning him round and wrenching his arm up behind his back. Together with another soldier, he marched the Doctor over to the jeep and shoved him roughly over the bonnet.

The Doctor gasped as his cheek pressed down on the hot metal. 'Ouch – careful!'

'This is a restricted area,' another soldier barked.

'I kind of guessed, actually.'

'What are you doing here? How did you get in?'

'I'm helping.' The Doctor forced himself upright. He raised his hands in the air and turned round. 'I've got papers, a pass, authorisation – everything.'

'Show me.'

'Rightio.' The Doctor shoved his hands into his jacket pockets. Except the pockets weren't there, and neither was the jacket. 'Ah. Sorry. Left my paper – my papers, I should say – in my jacket. I'd go and get it but it's a bit of a way away.'

'Gets hot out here,' one of the soldiers said. It was the first half-friendly tone the Doctor had heard. 'How far away's your jacket?'

'Quite a way, actually,' the Doctor admitted. 'I left it on the moon.'

It seemed like an age before anyone came. Amy

watched through a mass of pipes and cables. The soldier continued to stand in exactly the same spot, without moving at all.

'I have to stop doing this,' she muttered to herself in her hiding place. But it seemed safer to stay out of sight for now.

Eventually, Nurse Phillips arrived. She sighed when she saw the charred mass of fused cables and wires. She inspected the soldier's face, gently turning it from side to side.

'Come with me. We'd better get you to the medical centre.'

The soldier jerked upright at the sound of her voice. His shoulders straightened, his eyes opened again.

'Follow me. Let's get you sorted out.'

Since she knew where they were headed, Amy waited until they were long gone before she emerged from hiding.

By the time she had got to the medical centre – having taken several wrong turnings along the way – Nurse Phillips was bandaging the soldier's hand. He sat on a chair in the small reception area. His face was cleaner, but showed several slight burns. He seemed to be behaving perfectly normally as he glanced up at Amy and smiled. But there was no recognition in the look.

'What happened to you?' Amy asked.

'Oh, stupid accident. Burned my hand trying to fix a toasted sandwich.'

'Your face too, by the look of it.'

'Eye-level grill,' Nurse Phillips said. She finished

attaching the bandage with surgical tape. 'There, all done. Get a salad next time.'

'Sure thing.' The soldier stood up. 'Sorry to be a bother.'

'You remember what happened?' Amy asked.

Nurse Phillips frowned, but said nothing.

'Yeah,' the soldier said. 'Sure I do. Pretty much.'

'That's fine,' Nurse Phillips told him. 'A touch of shock, that's normal. You'll be all set in a day or two. No worries.'

'No worries,' the soldier repeated, his voice devoid of expression. Then happily, he added: 'Hey, I feel better already. Thanks.'

'Can I help you?' Nurse Phillips asked as soon as the soldier was gone.

'I thought maybe I could help you,' Amy said. 'I heard there was a soldier injured.'

'Oh?'

'One of the other men – saw him coming in, I guess. I didn't know how serious it was...'

'That's kind of you. But as you see, I'm managing fine.'

'As I see,' Amy agreed. 'Sorry, didn't mean to imply you couldn't cope.'

'It can be difficult with just me. Professor Jackson has some medical training, though, so that helps.'

'I'm sure it does,' Amy said.

One word changed everything. As soon as the Doctor mentioned the moon, the soldiers' demeanour changed completely. They helped him into the back of the jeep, and one even offered him chewing gum.

The Doctor declined.

'My spacesuit is about half a mile that way,' he explained. 'Any chance we can swing by and pick it up?'

'No problem,' the driver assured him.

The jeep sped away, kicking up a storm of fine sand behind it.

Half an hour later, with the Doctor's spacesuit (but not his helmet) duly recovered, they arrived back at Base Hibiscus. The base was made up of a collection of low brick-built structures. It looked every bit as incongruous sticking up from the desert as Base Diana had on the moon.

Guards on the gate waved the jeep through, and it screeched to a halt outside one of the low buildings. A sentry on duty outside glanced suspiciously at the Doctor before waving them all through. The interior of the building was more like an office than a military base. There were grey carpet tiles on the floor, and blotches of colour in expensive frames on the wall.

'You know,' the Doctor said, 'modern art isn't really as bad as it's painted.'

One of the soldiers was generous enough to smile. They continued in silence in the elevator to the third floor, where the Doctor was shown into an office. The door closed behind him, and he found himself facing an important-looking soldier across an imposing desk.

'I'm sorry if I'm supposed to know who you are,' the Doctor said, sitting down. 'General?' he hazarded, seeing the stars on the man's shoulders.

'General Walinski, and that's fine. I don't know

who you are either. Though that is a bit more of a problem, given I've recently checked the files of everyone who's supposed to be on Base Diana.'

'Guessing I wasn't on the list.'

'Damn right you weren't. So who are you, and how did you get there. More to the point, how did you get back?'

'Well, that's a little difficult really. I'm an expert, sent in to help. They're having a bit of trouble with their quantum link, though I expect you know that.'

'It's been noticed. Go on – you were sent to fix the link.'

'I *did* fix it. But then it went wrong again and dumped me back in the desert. Colonel Devenish...' The Doctor's voice tailed off.

Walinski leaned forward. 'Cliff Devenish – what about him?'

'He was with me, fixing the receptors. He didn't make it. I'm sorry.'

Walinski leaned back, nodding slowly. 'Good man, Devenish. So how come you made it back and he didn't? Chance, was it? Luck?'

'A bit of both, the Doctor admitted. 'And maybe I can survive a little longer without oxygen.'

Walinski leaned back in his chair. 'You see, the trouble I'm having here is that people are dead and you turn up out of nowhere and seem to be an expert on a top secret system. I don't know if I can trust you.'

The Doctor sucked in his cheeks. 'That's your problem not mine.'

'Don't be so sure.'

'Devenish trusted me, if that helps. At least, he told me he did.'

'You could be lying,' Devenish pointed out. 'Though you don't look like a liar.'

'Well,' the Doctor told him, 'good liars don't. But Devenish trusted me enough to agree when I told him the systems had been sabotaged.'

Walinski's eyes narrowed. 'How did you get to Diana?'

'My assistant Miss Pond and I went up from the shopping centre where the astronaut appeared.'

Walinski seemed to relax at this. 'Typical CIA. They sent their own team up – local Brit team, I guess – and they didn't even tell us.' He stood up, towering over the seated Doctor, and strode to the door. He pulled it open and shouted: 'Get Agent Jennings in here now.'

Jennings arrived almost at once. He was nearly as tall as Walinski, and just as broad. Unlike the General, Jennings was wearing a black suit. He was wearing glasses, and the lenses were as dark as the suit.

'This Doctor guy one of yours?' Walinski demanded.

'Not so far as I know.'

'Hi, by the way,' the Doctor said.

Jennings ignored him. 'But Control doesn't always consult me personally before putting agents into the field. You want me to double check?'

The Doctor stood up. 'Look, this is all very cosy and matey and fun, and we can play "my boss is bigger than your boss" for as long as you like. But my friend is up on your moonbase, and there's no way for us to get to her and there's no way for her to get to us. Whether you know it or not, something's sabotaging your systems. They deliberately cut you off from the moon, and they did that for a reason. Now I don't know what that reason is, not yet. But I think we should find out, don't you?'

'And why do you think someone would sabotage a base that's operated without problems for forty years?' Jennings asked.

'I didn't say some*one*, I said some*thing*.' The Doctor looked from Jennings to Walinski, and saw that they were both watching him closely. 'And I don't know why. But if I had to hazard a guess, and I think I'm probably more qualified than anyone else here to do that, then I'd say...' He hesitated, wondering if the two men would be ready for what he was about to tell them.

'Yes?' Walinski prompted.

'I'd say you're being invaded.'

Chapter
10

Captain Reeve had organised a room for Amy. She was tempted to tell him about what she'd seen and overheard. But when it came to it, she wasn't sure she could trust anyone. Captain Reeve seemed pleasant and friendly enough – certainly in contrast to Major Carlisle. But maybe he was just a bit too laid back. Could it all be an act? It was just typical of the Doctor to naff off and leave her on her own. When she saw him again he deserved a good slap.

'Looks like you could be staying with us for a while,' Reeve said.

'Any news of the Doctor and Devenish yet?' Amy asked.

'No. But it's a tricky job. The Colonel was on local comms only for some reason. Wasn't talking to us. That's not normal procedure. But they've got enough air for a few more hours yet, so Major Carlisle says we should leave them to it. They'll shout if they get a problem, or if they don't we'll go looking when their air gets low.'

'You seem to have a lot of spare living space,' Amy said, as much to change the subject as anything.

'The number of people stationed here varies. We have capacity at the moment.'

Amy nodded. She hadn't seen that many people. A few scientists in Jackson's team, Nurse Phillips, and the soldiers. 'How many here at the moment?'

'Maybe twenty in all. Major Carlisle could tell you the exact number.'

Reeve left her to 'settle in', though Amy wasn't sure what he thought she needed to do to settle in. It wasn't like she had anything to unpack. She lay on the bed and stared at the plain white ceiling. Not even a cobweb. Did they have spiders here in the base? Maybe some had wandered in through the quantum thingie, or come with the building materials. She closed her eyes, deciding she could doze for a few minutes. Just till the Doctor got back. He wouldn't be long.

She was woken what seemed like seconds later by a knocking at her door.

'What – who is it?'

'Downham, ma'am.'

Downham was a soldier. He stood to attention when Amy opened the door. 'Yes?'

'The Doctor would like to speak to you, ma'am.'

'You can cut the "ma'am" stuff. I'm Amy.'

'This way... miss.' He marched off down the corridor.

'So where are we going?' Amy asked, wondering

why the Doctor hadn't just come to find her himself.

'Communications Room.'

'And that's where the Doctor is?'

'Not exactly. You need to speak to him on the radio link. They're bouncing the signal off a couple of satellites so we can have voice contact.'

'Voice contact? Hang on – where exactly *is* the Doctor?'

The soldier hesitated in mid-stride, just slightly. 'Base Hibiscus. He's on Earth, ma'am.'

Captain Reeve was already talking on the radio when Amy arrived in the Communications Room.

'General Walinski, he's the officer in charge of Hibiscus,' Reeve said quietly to Amy. Louder he said: 'Sir, I have Miss Pond with me now, if the Doctor's still there.'

To Amy's surprise, the General ignored Reeve and kept talking:

'…which means that our number one priority must be to get the quantum displacement link operating again.' He paused, then went on: 'Glad to hear that, Reeve. The Doctor is just here.'

'He's a bit slow on the uptake,' Amy said quietly.

'There's a few seconds' delay,' Reeve explained. 'Should be more but your Doctor friend has done something to boost the signal, but there's still a delay before they hear us, and another before we hear their reply.'

'I had a teacher like that,' Amy told him.

'I'll give you guys some privacy,' Reeve said, 'I gather the Doctor wants to talk technical to you without us non-techies getting confused and interrupting.'

'I hope he wasn't too rude about it,' Amy called after Reeve as he left. He closed the door behind him, leaving Amy alone in the room.

'Pond – good to talk to you.' The Doctor's voice was slightly tinny over the speakers. 'Sorry I'm stuck down here. What do you mean?' he sounded suddenly offended. 'Of course I wasn't rude.'

'A few seconds' delay,' Amy said. 'This is going to be fun.'

'Now the first thing you need to know,' the Doctor said, 'is that there's a slight delay... Oh – you do know. So it'll be a few seconds before you hear my reply to your question.'

'Gotcha.'

'But I expect Reeve's clued you in, so you probably know that too, right?'

'I do.'

'What do you mean "Gotcha"? '

'No, no – that was last time. The Gotcha was for the slight delay bit.'

'Or was that your answer to the last question? Right, guessing it was... Ah, yes – you just said.'

Amy sighed. 'Look, is there some point to this conversation, or did you just call up to be all smug about having got back to Earth and left me stranded up here?'

The Doctor was talking at the same time: 'You're probably wondering why I've called, and it's not just me being smug about...' He hesitated, then went on: 'Oh, you are. Good.'

'Doctor,' Amy said, 'I'm guessing you have things

to tell me, and I certainly have things to tell you. So rather than getting behind each other all the time, why don't you go first?'

'Absolutely… Yes,' the Doctor said. Then, after a pause: 'You go first.'

'Me?'

'Oh, *I'm* going first?' The Doctor sounded surprised. 'OK, if you're sure.'

'I'm sure.'

'You want to go first? Is that what you mean by "Me"?'

'No, no it isn't.' Amy was getting exasperated.

'Sure you want to go first?' He paused, and Amy could imagine her voice coming out of the speakers back at the base in Houston. 'Good, off you go then.'

Obviously she was going to have to go first after all. But before she could start, the Doctor said:

'Sorry, what do you mean by "No it isn't?"'

'Doctor, just be quiet. Whatever you're saying, when you hear this just shut up and listen to me, OK?'

'I've obviously misunderstood,' the Doctor was saying. 'So let me tell you what's going on here, and you just won't *believe* what—' He broke off. 'Oh, all right then. Shutting up now. Off you go.'

Amy's hands were like claws in front of her, miming the action of wringing the absent Doctor's neck. She took a deep breath, then described what had happened to her. She told him about speaking to Liz Didbrook, and about seeing Nurse Phillips, Professor Jackson and Major Carlisle go into the Process Chamber. She described her fight with the soldier, and how he had just sort of switched off before being sent to the medical centre by Nurse Phillips.

'And there he was, having his hand bandaged as if nothing had happened. Well, nothing except he'd burned his hand. How can he *not* remember? And how can he think this is all normal? I mean, I know the military aren't always the sharpest tools in the box, but even soldiers must have some critical abilities. They have to be able to shoot guns, don't they? So you'd hope they can tell one end from the other at least. Maybe I've been overestimating—'

'Um, Amy?' the Doctor interrupted. 'I know you said not to interrupt, but just so you know, I've got General Walinski with me here still. And a couple of other military people. Sorry, should have mentioned that earlier. It might be a bit late to tell you that by the time you hear me.'

Amy closed her eyes and cringed inwardly. 'No but seriously,' she said quickly. 'I was just kidding, I think soldiers are great. Lovely… uniforms. Sorry, Doctor, what was that? Oh and a great sense of humour too, so they'll know what I mean.'

There was an awkward pause that seemed to last for ever. Then a voice Amy recognised as the General from his conversation with Captain Reeve earlier said levelly: 'That was a long few seconds.'

'Longest of my life,' Amy muttered. Louder, she went on: 'Anyway, that's what's been happening to me. So, basically, I guess the soldier's mind was affected somehow, and it has to be to do with Jackson's process. Mind-wipes and all that. It was like he'd been hypnotised or programmed or something.

Anyone could be affected, I don't know who to trust.'
As she said it, she realised just how alone she was. 'I
miss you, Doctor. When are you coming back? I need
you here.'

There was another long pause. Then the Doctor's
voice came through:

'My turn now, then, if you've finished. What?
Oh, yes, I miss you too. Coming back? Well, slight
problem there because the quantum link needs to be
mended at your end. And I don't think there's anyone
up there who can do it. Or at least, no one who wants
to.'

'You've confirmed Colonel Devenish's sabotage
theory,' Walinski said. 'Though we still don't have a
motive, unless the Doctor's right.'

Right about what? Amy almost asked. But she bit
her tongue and kept quiet.

Sure enough, the Doctor explained anyway.
'You're spot on about Jackson's process,' he said. 'I
don't know if Jackson is behind it, but the process has
been hijacked. You remember I said that there's a void
left by removing the patient's memories? And it needs
to be filled with something else? I think that's what's
happening. Something has found the empty spaces
and sneaked in. Maybe that's how these "Blanks" you
mentioned are being programmed and controlled. Or
perhaps that's a separate application of the process.
But something is fixing on the blank spaces in the
mind and taking up residence there.'

'You mean, like downloading software onto a
blank bit of hard disk, of computer memory?' Amy
asked. 'Sorry,' she added quickly.

'I wish I could think of a good analogy,' the Doctor went on, oblivious. 'Something went wrong with that poor Prisoner Nine, and Jackson put some of his own memories into the man's brain. That was how he knew *me*, and how he recalled setting up the process in the first place. What Jackson does is he erases a bit of someone's memory, and into that space...' He paused. 'Yes...' He paused again. 'Oh that's very good, yes. That's exactly what it's like. *Downloading*, I like that. Actually, I don't like it at all, but the analogy is good.'

'So who's downloading stuff into people's brains?' Amy asked.

'The question is who's downloading stuff into people's brains,' Walinski said.

'You both think so,' the Doctor said. 'Well, the answer is – I don't know. But it's something that has an affinity with the human brain. Something that can transmit into the mind itself. Something that has a purpose in doing just that. Something that definitely *isn't* human.'

'And that has hostile intentions,' Walinski added.

'Seems that way,' the Doctor agreed. 'Hold tight, Amy. I'm going to try to fix things from down here. I'll find a way to reconnect long enough for me to get back, then I can sort out the alien invaders, and we can all go home. Easy.'

'Oh yeah, easy,' Amy said. Even over the radio, she could tell from his tone that the Doctor was more worried than he was letting on.

'Just make sure no one else gets to find out about this,' the Doctor said. 'You're right not to trust anyone… Oh, glad you think so. But it probably *won't* be so easy…'

In another room on Base Diana, the Doctor's voice came clearly through a small speaker wired into the main communications systems.

'I'll talk to you again soon. If you need to call us, you can talk to the General here, or Agent Jennings. Or you can ask for Candace Hecker. She's in charge of research and… stuff. So she'll know what you're talking about. Probably. As much as anyone, anyway. Just sit tight till I sort something out.'

The uniformed figure in the room reached out and turned off the speaker. The Doctor was a problem, even stranded back on Earth. They would have to make sure he never got back to the moon.

answer. 'Oh, yes...do think so. But it probably won't be scary.'

In another room, on base, Diana, the Director's voice came clearly through a small speaker wired into the ...communications systems.

'I think, by you again soon, L. you need to call us, you can talk to the Control here, or Agent Jennings. Or you can ask for Candace here, she's here to draw a ...research and... well, so she'll know what you're talking about. Probably as much as anyone anyway, just enough till something, OK.'

The uniformed man in the room reached out and turned off the speaker. The Earth, was a problem, even stranded back on Earth, they would have to make sure he'd even get back to the moon.

Chapter
11

Of one thing, Amy was sure – she wasn't going to 'just sit tight' until the Doctor sorted something out. That might be days – or weeks, even. And for all she knew, the bad guys – Jackson or the aliens, if there were actually any aliens – were already suspicious of her. According to the Doctor, they'd tried to kill him, and had actually killed Colonel Devenish, just for interfering.

She didn't doubt for a moment that the Doctor *would* be back. He wouldn't abandon her. He wouldn't abandon the TARDIS either, which was parked out on the lunar surface. When he did get back, it would be useful to know who they could trust, and who'd had their mind fried and occupied by the alien invaders.

One encouraging thing was that the Doctor's theory made sense of some of the things that Liz Didbrook had said. In between the gibberish and rubbish, she'd talked about 'them'. Even the poor prisoner who'd died after being processed had warned: 'They're here.' Was that Jackson himself, his mind free of the alien influence, trying to warn them through someone else's body?

Amy was sure that she couldn't trust either Jackson, Nurse Phillips or Major Carlisle – not that she liked the Major anyway. But there was no one, not even the ever-attentive and charming Captain Reeve, that she was sure she *could* trust. No one except Liz Didbrook. And Amy could only trust her in those brief moments when she slipped nuggets of information and words of warning between the random sentences that perhaps kept the aliens in her mind at bay. If she'd been an early victim of the process, maybe it had gone wrong or not worked properly on her...

Without having really made a decision, Amy found she was walking towards the Medical Centre. If Liz was possessed by some alien mind parasite then it already knew about Amy's interest. Talking to her again could hardly make things worse.

Hoping she was right, Amy peered carefully round the door to the Medical Centre. She'd rather Nurse Phillips didn't know she'd come back for another chat with the star patient.

Nurse Phillips was standing at her desk in the small reception area. The fact that she was standing up was hopeful. Unless she'd just arrived and was about to sit down... Amy waited, hardly daring to breath, and ready to duck back out of sight if Nurse Phillips looked towards the door. But she seemed intent on something on the desk. She reached down, and turned a sheet of paper. She was reading something –

a medical report probably.

After what seemed an age, Nurse Phillips straightened up, checked her watch, and then headed purposefully towards the door.

Amy quickly ran back down the corridor. She hadn't thought about what to do if Nurse Phillips actually left. She'd hoped the woman would go through into the main part of the Medical Centre to check on someone or something so she could slip inside and get to Liz Didbrook.

Amy opened the nearest door and hurried inside. The room was dark, and Amy quickly pushed the door almost shut behind her. She left a crack of light, watching until Nurse Phillips had walked past. Then Amy breathed a heavy sigh of relief. She was about to open the door again when the lights came on.

'Holy Moley!' a gruff voice announced. 'Who are *you*?'

Amy spun round. She was in a bedroom, identical to the one Captain Reeve had assigned to her. Except that this was not her bedroom. And the soldier it did belong to was sitting up in bed, metal dogtags rattling against his bare chest.

'Oh, er hi,' Amy said. 'Health and Safety, just checking your door. Making sure the hinges don't squeak. In the dark.' She opened and closed the door a couple of times just to show. 'See. No problem.'

The soldier didn't look convinced. In fact he looked rather irritated – angry even. He swung his bare legs out of the bed, and as the sheets looked about to fall away, Amy pulled the door open and hurried out into the corridor. 'Give yourself an A1 rating for your hinges,' she called back. 'Sorry to disturb you.'

There was a quiet, steady blip from the equipment. Liz was asleep, breathing regularly and calmly. Amy hoped she wasn't heavily sedated. She shook the young woman's shoulder gently. Then more firmly.

After several seconds, Liz's eyes flickered open. 'What? Is it time for milk and honey?'

'It's me, Amy. I spoke to you before, remember?'

'Memory cheats,' Liz said sleepily. 'Other people's memories are not their own.'

'I know – I know what you mean now. I know why you have to speak nonsense. It's to stop them getting a hold in your mind, so they don't realise that you're telling me things, isn't it?'

'I tried to tell everyone. I put a wolf in the wood.'

'A spanner in the works? Is that what you mean?'

'A fly in the ointment.'

'You mean the sabotage?' Amy was talking in a loud whisper, though she was pretty sure there was no one else about. '*You* sabotaged the systems, is that what you're saying?'

'Neglected children seek it. Soldiers stand to it.'

'What?'

'An elastic band gets stretched and has it.'

It wasn't nonsense at all, Amy realised. More like a code, and she was just beginning to get the hang of it. 'A tension. You mean attention – you sabotaged the systems to get attention? Well, you got me and the Doctor, so it sort of worked.'

Suddenly Liz sat up. 'Have you come to take me to the party? Will I see all the others now? I'm sleepy. I could go to the party. The sleepover party. All sleeping.'

'What party?' Amy asked. 'What do you mean?'

'Or am I too sleepy?' The woman slumped backwards on to her pillow. Her grey eyes closed. 'You go for me. At quarter past nine, or just after. 21.17 it opens. But don't sleep over. Never sleep over. Waking is best. Gatecrashers not wanted, oh no. Naughty.'

'OK,' Amy said. 'Seriously confused now. So, where is this party you want me to gatecrash?' She put her hand on Liz's shoulder. 'Where?'

The eyes snapped open again – vivid blue irises staring at Amy. 'Pod 7,' Liz said. 'Party on.' Then her eyes closed again, and she began to snore softly.

The woman in the reception area of the Medical Centre turned sharply as Amy walked in.

'Oh, it's you,' Amy said. 'I don't think Nurse Phillips is here, I was just looking for her.'

'No problem,' Major Carlisle said shortly. 'You know how long she'll be?'

Amy shook her head. 'She wasn't here when I arrived.'

'You and the Doctor – why are you *really* here?'

'To fix the systems.' It came out like a question. Amy sensed she was being interrogated.

'I just wonder if I can trust you,' Major Carlisle said.

'Oh absolutely. Very trustworthy. Something you want to confess?' Maybe that was going too far, Amy thought. But she'd said it now.

'Tell me,' Carlisle said slowly, 'have you noticed

anything odd since you arrived here on Diana?'

'Apart from the fact the quantum thing isn't working.'

'Not the equipment, the people.' Major Carlisle stared intently at Amy, as if trying to read the answer in her freckles.

'The people?' This must be a trick. How Amy answered could mean the difference between life and death, liberty and... being processed. 'No, everyone's been very good and helpful. Why do you ask?'

Major Carlisle's eyes narrowed slightly. 'No reason. Just that I want to be sure my team is giving you all the help and attention you need.'

'Oh yes,' Amy assured her. 'I'm getting all the attention I need.' Then, as Major Carlisle turned to leave, Amy said: 'What's in Pod 7?'

Carlisle paused, then turned back. 'Why do you ask?'

'Just wondered. Something someone said.'

'Someone?'

'One of your team.'

Major Carlisle nodded as if this made sense. 'Pod 7 is a holding and processing area for new prisoners. We've had none for several months and none are due – even before the current transportation problems.'

'So, what's in there?'

'Nothing. Pod 7 is completely empty.' Carlisle tilted her head slightly to one side. 'Does that answer your question, Miss Pond?'

'It does, thank you, Major Carlisle.'

'Then I'll leave you to it.'

*

120

'Stupid, stupid, stupid,' Amy muttered to herself over and over. It was stupid to have asked about Pod 7 and tipped Major Carlisle off like that. Of course she'd given nothing away. But then again, maybe she'd think that Amy believed her – why wouldn't she, after all?

Amy had headed to the canteen and got herself a coffee – that tasted foul. She was pretty sure she wasn't being followed. Major Carlisle had gone off towards the admin area. Pod 7 was on the other side of the base. Well away from everything else, it was a separate area extending out from the main part of the base. That made sense if it was where the prisoners arrived. Isolated and self-contained. But it also meant there was only one corridor leading to it.

To get to that one corridor, Amy had to pass the cell block. She stared out at the central hub, knowing now that there were people incarcerated there. The door at the far end of the long room was locked, a numeric keypad beside it. There was also a small, square glass plate like a fire alarm activator. Amy was tempted to break the plate, but it would probably set off an alarm and there was no guarantee it would unlock the door. And who knew what else it might do?

But she didn't know the code. Or did she? Liz had said the party was at 21.17, which had seemed like an odd time even for an imaginary party. What exactly had she said? '21.17 it opens.' That had to be it. Amy keyed in 2117, and the door slid open.

'Yes!' Amy said in triumph. Immediately, she turned to check there was no one there.

Amy let the door close behind her, then keyed the

code in again to make sure she could get out. Happy that it worked both ways, she let the door close once more, then made her way cautiously along the corridor to Pod 7.

The light gradually dimmed as she went along the corridor, augmented at first and eventually replaced by the blood-red glow of the emergency lighting. Amy guessed that as the area wasn't used, they didn't bother keeping the lights on all the time.

If it really wasn't used.

The corridor ended in another door. Again, Amy keyed in the 2117 code. Again, the door slid silently open. And Amy stepped into a nightmare.

There were twenty tables, arranged in four rows of five and all illuminated by the eerie red lighting. Each table was about two metres long by a metre wide, all identical, plain, plastic and metal like you might find in a modern office.

Except that lying on each table was a body. Wires ran from pads attached to the bodies' temples to a monitor beside each table. Heartbeats blipped across a small screen. Temperatures rose and fell by fractions of a degree. All twenty bodies breathed to the same rhythm, so that the room itself sounded as if it was alive.

Amy walked slowly between the rows of tables. What was this place? A sick bay, or something more sinister?

All twenty bodies were wearing army uniforms. They were mostly men, but there were a few women too. All twenty had their eyes wide open, and all were staring sightlessly at the ceiling.

All except the soldier on the table closest to the door where Amy had come in. He was staring right at Amy as she moved along the rows of tables. The blip of his heartbeat went dead and his temperature fell, as he pulled the pads from his head and sat up.

Chapter
12

The hot Texan sun reflected off the polished metal plates like they were mirrors. Candace Hecker watched Graham Haines repositioning one of the plates. Other scientists were checking the angles and connections of the other plates.

For once, Agent Jennings' sunglasses didn't seem out of place as he stood with General Walinski watching the work. Feeling both unnecessary and out of her depth, Candace joined them. She wasn't used to feeling this way, and she didn't like it.

'Will this work?' Walinski asked.

Candace shrugged. 'Who knows? No one really understands how quantum displacement works, not since Charlie Flecknoe died.'

'He set the systems up?' Jennings asked.

Candace nodded. 'Invented it, built the equipment, got it working. Then got cancer and was dead in months. That was back in the eighties. He left loads of notes, but only a few people understand any of them. It's been enough to keep the systems working, but we've really been operating on a wing and a prayer.'

'And now the wing's bust,' Walinski told them. 'But this Doctor – he seems to understand it.'

'He doesn't look old enough to know diddly,' Jennings said.

They watched the Doctor in his shirtsleeves running between the metal plates that ran in two parallel lines across the desert. He realigned some, checked the wires connecting others. Sometimes just nodded his appreciation.

'He looks older when he's busy,' Walinski said. 'There's no question he knows his stuff. I mean, he can't be bluffing can he?'

'His equations are brilliant and correct,' Candace said. 'His theory seems sound. He certainly understands the principles involved. He's...' She struggled to think of a less emotive word, but couldn't. 'He's a genius,' she admitted. 'But even he says there's no guarantee this will work.'

'So what's supposed to happen?' Jennings asked.

The Doctor came running up to them in time to hear the question. 'The whole theory's bonkers,' he said. 'So probably nothing. But if I can resonate the plates at the same frequency as the receptors on the moon, that might establish an affinity between the two locations so they overlap again.'

'You can fix it?' Walinski said.

'In about three months with unlimited funding and resources, like the people who set it up – of course I can. No problem. But today? Well, sort of, maybe, a bit. Most likely it won't work at all. Or if it does, it won't be stable.'

'So, forgive me, but what's the point?' asked Jennings.

'There's always a chance it will work. You've got to try,' Candace told him.

'Absolutely,' the Doctor agreed. He pulled a roll of paper from his pocket – Candace could see it was a sheaf of pages torn from a notebook and covered with handwritten scribbles. 'It might not be safe for any of us to go through, but I've written some thoughts on how the systems can be repaired at the moonbase end. Assuming they want to repair them. But the advantage of paper is that it won't suffocate if it's left out on the moon.' He stuffed the notes back in his pocket. 'Now I have a question,' he said to Jennings.

'Yeah?'

'Aren't you hot in that suit?'

It was even hotter inside the spacesuit. The Doctor found the close-fitting white cotton balaclava even more claustrophobic and stifling.

'I'd rather be in my own spacesuit; it's not so cumbersome,' he complained.

'I don't know where you got it,' Candace told him, 'but you've lost the helmet, and ours don't fit. I'm looking forward to reverse-engineering the thing.'

'Don't you dare. Not so much as a stitch of it.'

'But—' she started to protest.

The Doctor put his hand up. 'Ah!' he warned. 'End of.'

With everyone cleared well out of the way, the

Doctor stood at the end of the path formed between the rows of reflective metal plates. He operated the control on the side of his helmet that lowered the gold-tinted visor, blocking out the glare.

He held up his sonic screwdriver in a bulky, gloved hand. 'Well, here we go,' he murmured.

The tip of the screwdriver glowed into life. There was a hum of power from the generators attached to the plates. He adjusted the screwdriver setting slightly to alter the frequency. The air in front of the Doctor was shimmering with the heat. But maybe also with something else.

Between the lines of plates, the sky darkened. The sand was drained of colour – grey and barren. A wind blew past the Doctor as air rushed into the area where there had been a vacuum, filling the path between the receptors on the moon.

'Oh yes,' the Doctor announced. But his glee was tempered when he saw the figure swimming into existence in front of him.

Colonel Devenish's ravaged face stared back at the Doctor from where he lay on the surface of the moon. His gloved hand stretched out, as if pleading for help – help that had never come.

It was like walking into a storm, as if the air was rushing out again. The Doctor leaned into it, struggling forwards.

'What's happening?' Candace Hecker's voice asked inside his helmet. 'Is it working?'

'Yes and no,' the Doctor gasped as he stumbled onwards. 'The displacement won't hold for long. If I'm inside the area when it fails, I'll be ripped apart.

The local geography's trying to reassert itself.'

'Just leave your papers and get out.'

The Doctor had his sheaf of papers in his free hand. He pressed them down on the dusty ground close to Devenish's body. He could feel the papers fighting to escape and blow away. He needed to weigh them down, but even then they might be ripped apart when the displacement bubble burst.

Devenish's space helmet was close by – achingly close to the dead man's hand. The Doctor rolled it on top of the papers. The helmet trembled in the gale, but stayed put. Then the Doctor took Devenish's outstretched hand.

'I'm sorry,' he murmured. 'I never meant to leave you here to die, and I'm not leaving you to get ripped apart now.' The wind was with him as he dragged the man's body back into the Texan desert.

Close by, lay another space helmet – red and gleaming. The Doctor stretched out a leg awkwardly, and kicked the helmet ahead of him. It rolled like tumbleweed across the cold lunar surface and out into the shimmering heat of the desert.

The Doctor followed after it, dragging Colonel Devenish's body. As soon as he was clear of the line of metal plates, he sank to his knees.

Behind him, the plates exploded, one after another, all along the lines. Between them, a trail of stumbling footmarks and the path of a dragged body started abruptly, then led out of the pathway to where the Doctor was struggling out of his spacesuit.

'So close,' Candace said, running over to him. 'We almost did it. If only the link had stabilised.'

'History is full of "if only"s,' the Doctor told her sadly. 'That was our last chance. Our last way back to the moon.' He pulled off a glove and hurled it to the ground.

General Walinski was standing beside Candace Hecker. The two of them exchanged looks.

'No,' Walinski said to her. 'Absolutely not.'

'What?' the Doctor asked. 'Tell me.'

'You said we'd lost our last chance to get back to the moon,' Candace said. Walinski sighed and looked down at the sandy desert floor as she went on: 'There might just be another way.'

The soldier's attention was fixed on Amy. He swung his legs over the side of the table in a single fluid movement and stood up.

'Nearest the door, so you must be the guard,' Amy said.

The soldier didn't reply. He looked to be about the same age as Amy, with close-cropped fair hair. He walked calmly and purposefully towards her.

Amy backed away, keeping several tables between them. The soldier changed course, moving between tables, but always blocking Amy's route to the door.

'Tell you what, I'll just be going. I can let myself out.'

The soldier didn't seem to have heard. He was focused intently on Amy. As he got closer, his hands reached out – like a zombie in a cheap movie. Except that film zombies usually lumbered and lurched slowly after their victims. This guy was walking briskly and with determination.

Amy ran down a line of tables, cutting back into the next row. The soldier matched her, running parallel along the other side of the tables, and cutting through so he was in the next aisle.

What if she stopped, and waited to see which way he went? Would the soldier just switch off, like the other one had done?

She tried it. They faced each other over the prone body of a young woman in army fatigues.

'You just going to stand there all day?' Amy asked.

As if in answer, the soldier leaned forward, both hands on the edge of the table. Then in a single movement, he vaulted across the table and the body lying on it, landing right beside Amy.

She gave a shriek of surprise, instantly embarrassed by it, and ran.

The soldier was no longer between her and the door. But he was right next to her. His hand grabbed Amy's hair, jerking her back as she moved.

'Get off!' she yelled.

But the soldier held on, dragging Amy back towards him.

In desperation she kicked backwards at him, hoping to slam her foot into his shin. Instead it caught the low pedestal beside the bed. The impact jarred right up through her leg, making her eyes water as much as the pain from having her hair pulled.

The pedestal rocked as she kicked it. The equipment slid across the top, and crashed to the floor. Wires stretched and tangled. A connection broke loose. An alarm sounded – an insistent low buzzer.

And, suddenly, Amy was free. The soldier let go of her hair. She was so surprised she didn't move. The soldier quickly but carefully lifted the equipment back onto the pedestal and reconnected the loose wire. The buzzer stopped. The soldier turned back towards Amy. His hands shot out again, but this time she managed to duck out of reach. She turned and ran – the soldier close behind her. His booted footsteps echoing in her ears as he closed on her.

The door was so far away. Amy dodged round tables, raced along the aisles between them. But the soldier was right behind her. She felt his hand brush against her shoulder as he grabbed for her. Knew that before she reached the door, he would catch up with her. And when he did…

Gasping for breath, she ran faster. Past the table where the soldier chasing her had been sleeping. Just one row of tables between Amy and the door now.

Then her foot caught on the trailing wires that the soldier had pulled from his own temple and discarded. She slipped, stumbled, almost regained her balance. Fell.

The back of Amy's head crashed into the floor. The ceiling above her shimmered and blurred. She stared up into the empty grey eyes of the solder as his hands reached down and closed round her neck.

Chapter

13

Amy didn't give the soldier a chance to tighten his grip. She rolled out of the way, breaking his grip. As she rolled, she kicked out at the nearest pedestal, sending equipment flying. As soon as she was on her feet, she ran – not for the door, but from bed to bed, ripping electrodes off the sleepers' temples and pushing over the monitoring equipment.

The soldier set about picking up the monitors and reattaching the connections. He was meticulous and efficient. This was obviously a higher priority than chasing intruders.

'So it's your job to keep them safe,' Amy said. 'But safe for what?'

She watched the soldier reconnect another sleeper. The monitor blipped back into life. Temperature readings and blood pressure numbers rose to what Amy assumed was normal. She backed slowly away, not taking her eyes off the soldier as he worked. Would he decide she was a priority if he saw her escaping?

The door had slid shut behind her when she came in. She had to turn to see the numbers on the pad. It took her only a few seconds to key in the code, but she expected the soldier to be standing right there with her when she looked back.

He was still resetting the equipment on the other side of the room. She'd done it. She was safe.

Behind Amy, the door slid silently open.

She turned to leave. Just as a hand came down on her shoulder, gripping her tight.

'What are you doing here?'

They shared the back of a jeep back to Base Hibiscus – the Doctor, Candace, General Walinski and Agent Jennings. The Doctor was nursing his spacesuit helmet. Neither Walinski nor Candace Hecker had elaborated on their suggestion he could still get back to the moon. Was there an emergency back-up system? Something so dangerous they didn't dare use it?

'We still have no proof,' Walinski said above the sound of the engine, 'that your theory about alien invaders has any validity. It's a bit wild, to say the least.'

'The best theories are,' the Doctor told him. 'But whether I'm right or not, we need to re-establish a link with your base.'

'It's a question of urgency,' Hecker said. 'The technicians on Diana will be working on it. Jackson's brilliant. If anyone can fix this, he can.'

'So, what if anyone *can't* fix this?' Jennings shrugged. 'Just playing devil's advocate. But maybe no one can sort it, not even Jackson. And maybe – just maybe – the Doctor here is right. It doesn't have to be aliens, but if someone is sabotaging the systems at the moonbase end, it won't matter how brilliant Jackson is.'

'Who do you think might be behind the damage?' the Doctor asked. He sensed Jennings wasn't convinced it was extraterrestrials.

'Hell, we've locked up a lot of dangerous and unpleasant people there, Doc. Any one of them could have friends willing to die to get them free, or even just to make a point.'

'He's a dwarf,' the Doctor said. 'Do I look like a dwarf?'

Jennings frowned. 'The saboteur? You mean he had to fit into some small space to access the systems?'

'No, no, no. *Doc* is a dwarf. I'm not.' The Doctor stood up in the jeep, swaying as it moved, to make the point. There was an especially violent jolt as they crested a sand dune, and he sat down again. 'Sleepy, Sneezy, Dozy, Mick and Titch.' He stopped, biting his lower lip as he thought about this. 'No, hang on, that's not right, is it. Sleepy, Sneezy, Dopey, Grumpy, Happy, Bashful – doesn't end in "ee" but I'm sure that's right, after all he's another mood, isn't he?'

'And Doc,' Candace put in. 'That's right.'

'Doc's not a mood,' the Doctor said. 'Which always worried me, but he is definitely diminutive. And I'm not. So don't call me Doc, OK – Agent *Jenn*?'

Jennings laughed. 'Sure thing, *Doctor*. Though if you meet anyone as pretty as Snow White, you let me know where to find her, OK?'

'She's on the moon,' the Doctor said. 'And I'm going to get her back.'

Graham Haines was already waiting for them when they arrived back at Base Hibiscus. He was all but bouncing up and down with excitement.

'The scans the Doctor set running before you left – they've finished. It's incredible,' he told Candace.

'What's incredible?' Walinski demanded, jumping down from the jeep to join them.

'What he's done to the Herschel telescope for one thing, and all by remote control.' Haines shook his head in admiration. 'The man's a genius.'

'Course he is,' the Doctor said, striding swiftly past them. 'So let's see what Herschel has to show us, shall we?'

Walinski, Jennings, Candace Hecker and Haines all crammed into the General's office along with the Doctor. Haines had routed the scan results through to the Walinski's computer screen.

'Not bad for a dwarf,' Agent Jennings murmured quietly.

'Excuse me?' Haines was looking confused.

'It just looks like a load of bright colours against a dark background,' Walinski said. 'Someone care to tell me what it actually means?'

'It means the Doctor's right,' Candace said.

'It means trouble,' the Doctor added.

'These orange sections, like the stripes in a rainbow,' Candace explained, 'they're bursts of energy. This is calibrated like an MRI scanner. Magnetic Resonance, like you get in the brain.'

'It detects brain waves,' Haines said. 'In simple terms,' he added, catching a glare from Candace.

'And where are these brain waves?'

'We can't tell where they're coming from,' the Doctor said. 'But the point of arrival here...' He pointed to the end of the rainbow stripe. 'That's your Base Diana. Specifically, it's Professor Jackson's Process Chamber.'

There was silence for a while as they all stared at the rainbow pattern on the screen.

'Is this happening all the time?' Agent Jennings asked.

'No, it comes in bursts,' Haines said. 'But, get this – the bursts coincide with the logged schedule for use of the process equipment. It drains the power, so they have to log it,' he explained.

'Jackson fires up his machine,' the Doctor said, 'and alien brain waves zoom in at exactly the same moment. Time and again. It's not a coincidence.'

'And it's getting worse,' Candace told them. 'While Haines was putting through the data feed, I took a look at the back end of this rainbow of ours. Zoomed the Herschel as far out as it will go. This is real time, people.'

She worked at Walinski's keyboard for a few moments. The image on the screen was replaced by a strobing pattern of red light across the darkness.

'That is constant,' Jennings said. 'Right?'

'Right,' Candace agreed. 'Not controlled bursts any more, but a constant stream. The good news is it hasn't hit Diana yet – this is all upstream. But it's on its way, whatever it is.'

'Reinforcements,' the Doctor said. 'Downloading, remember? So far they've been sending bursts of mental activity. Like one alien brain at a time. Think of it like copying files to a CD, one after another.'

'And this?' Walinski tapped the screen.

'This is a constant download. This is a heap more data all coming at once. They just increased their bandwidth so they can send more than one brain at a time.'

'How many are we talking about?' Jennings wondered.

The Doctor shrugged. 'One each for everyone on Base Diana to begin with.'

'To begin with?' Haines whistled. 'What then?'

'Then one each for everyone on Earth.' The Doctor looked round at the grim faces of the others. 'They've accelerated their plans, stepped up a gear. Perhaps this was always their intention. Or maybe something's frightened them into thinking they have to move more quickly. That's why they cut the link. That's why this...' He pointed at the screen. '... is on its way. Once they have their reinforcements they'll reconnect the link and come through to Earth in force. We're running out of time.'

'But why? What could have frightened them so much they've changed their plans?' Walinski asked.

The Doctor grinned suddenly. 'Me. They know I can stop them. But I can't do it from here. I have to get back to the moon, and I think you know a way I can get there.'

Haines saw the look between Walinski and Candace Hecker. 'You cannot be serious,' he said. 'Tell me you're not thinking what I think you're thinking.'

'Doctor,' Walinski said, 'we need to show you something.'

The soldier had almost finished reconnecting all the sleepers to the equipment. Amy and Captain Reeve stood in the open doorway. Reeve watched in astonishment.

'It's Private Dyson,' Reeve said. 'He's supposed to be back at Hibiscus. In fact, all of these guys are. What are they still doing here?'

'I'm guessing your guys at Hibiscus think they're still up here going about their normal duties,' Amy said. 'Someone's been lying. Using your own secrecy against you to cover up what's really happening. Come on, we have to get out of here. Once he's finished, he's programmed to come after us.'

'Programmed?' Reeve shook his head, bewildered. It was almost comical to see the oh-so-cool Captain confused and astounded. 'What do you mean? These people are sick. We have to help them.'

'Yes, we do.' Amy pushed him back through the door into the corridor beyond. 'But we can't do it on our own. And we have to know who's behind this.'

'Nurse Phillips must know they're here.'

'I'm sure she does.' The door slid shut. 'Hang on.' Amy turned to stare at Reeve. 'How did you know I was in here?'

'I was in the security control room. I saw the door to the holding area had been opened. There was no authorisation, so I came to check.'

'They must have a way of overriding that when

they need to come here, so no one detects it.'

'But who?' Reeve asked.

Amy was hurrying back down the corridor. 'Nurse Phillips, and Professor Jackson.'

'*Jackson's* in on this too? What's going on?'

They reached the end of the corridor and Amy keyed open the door.

'It's kind of difficult to explain.'

'Try me.'

'Look, Professor Jackson's process removes memories from the human brain. I think those people in there have had their brains wiped completely clean. Jackson talked about "Blanks" – that's what they are. Literally, waiting to have a new personality imprinted into the empty brain.'

'You mean, like a mind-swap?'

'Yeah. Except the Doctor thinks that whatever is going to take over their brains is alien.'

Reeve laughed. 'You're kidding, right?' He stopped laughing as Amy glared at him. 'OK, not kidding. So what do you suggest we do about this?'

'Arrest Jackson and Nurse Phillips.' Amy turned to look out of the huge window at the central hub containing the cells. 'At least you've got somewhere to keep them. Solitary confinement.'

Reeve nodded slowly. 'I'll have to clear it with Major Carlisle. She might take a bit of convincing.'

'No!' Amy said sharply. 'I think she's in on this, too.'

'Andi Carlisle? No way!' Reeve gave a sudden snort of laughter. 'She's not an alien, she's always like that.'

'We can't risk it,' Amy insisted. 'Just you and me for now, till we find out more.'

'How do we do that?'

'From Jackson and Phillips.'

Reeve nodded. 'Makes sense. We'll go to my quarters first though, there's something I think we'll need.'

'Handcuffs?'

Reeve shook his head. 'Gun. Come on, let's do this. And whatever happens there's going to be hell to pay, so pray that you're right.'

'No,' Amy told him. 'Pray that I'm wrong.'

Chapter
14

There were just the four of them in the jeep – the Doctor, Candace Hecker, Agent Jennings, and General Walinski.

The General had insisted on driving. Candace was in the passenger seat beside him.

'I don't want anyone else knowing we even thought about this, unless we have to do it,' Walinski told her as they pulled out of the base.

A cloud of sand followed their progress, thrown up by the wheels as they sped across the empty desert. There were no landmarks, no signs, no road even. But Walinski seemed to know exactly where they were going.

'You know this is crazy,' Candace told him.

Walinski nodded. 'Crazy may be all we have left, Candace.'

Jennings and the Doctor were sitting in the back of the jeep.

'You know what they're talking about?' Jennings asked.

'I can make a pretty good guess,' the Doctor admitted happily. He was grinning like a kid in a candy store. 'You?'

'Nope. Crazy, that I understand, but nothing else. Hey – this whole thing is crazy, start to finish.'

'It's not finished yet,' the Doctor said, his expression clouding over.

'Tell me, are you serious about these aliens? I mean, *seriously* serious?'

'Very seriously serious. Though I do notice you and the General haven't been kicking up a fuss and insisting there's no such thing as alien life or the whole idea is complete nonsense.'

Jennings took off his sunglasses and polished them on a spotless white handkerchief before replacing them.

'I guess Walinski's read some of the same files I have. UNIT, Torchwood, Operation Yellow Book – the real deal, not the sanitised cover-up stuff they put out under Freedom of Information.'

'UNIT?' the Doctor said. 'You know who *I* am, then?'

Jennings smiled thinly. 'I would if you were a good deal older.'

'Believe me,' the Doctor told him, 'I'm a good deal older.'

They drove for about an hour, the sun scorching down from a clear blue sky. Finally, in the distance, the Doctor could make out something that wasn't just more sand.

Jennings had seen it too. 'What is that? It looks like a building. A spire of some sort.'

The Doctor didn't answer, but his grin was back.

As they got closer, the shape resolved itself through the shimmering heat into a tall, circular, white tower. It tapered at the top, ending in a sharp-looking spike that thrust up into the sky.

'It's still a long way off,' Jennings said. 'Is that where we're headed?' he called out to Walinski. 'Not that there's anything else out here,' he said to the Doctor.

But the Doctor wasn't listening. He was intent on the growing structure ahead of them, gleaming in the sunlight.

The jeep bumped up a sharp incline, like the edge of a crater. It was now apparent that the structure was far taller than just the section visible above the edge of the 'crater'. The ground dropped away into a vast open bowl scooped out of the desert.

Walinski stopped the vehicle at the rim, throwing up clouds of sand as he skidded to a halt.

'You are *so* kidding me,' Jennings said, leaping out of the back of the jeep.

The Doctor was bouncing on the balls of his feet with enthusiasm. 'That is... fantastic,' he decided. 'Brilliant. Fab, if I can use a very sixties word – and I think under the circumstances I can.'

The four of them stood at the edge of the 'crater' looking across at the enormous structure.

'It always gets me,' Walinski confessed. 'I don't come out here often, but every time I do I'm just staggered by the sheer size of it. The engineering that went into *that*.'

'Three hundred and sixty-three feet tall,' Candace said.

'That's about the same as St Paul's Cathedral,' the Doctor said. 'What's she weigh?'

'Fully fuelled, over three thousand tonnes.'

'That is one hell of a thing,' Jennings said.

Below them, several low buildings were clustered round the edge of the crater. They were well away from the main structure in the middle, though roads had been built between them. Huge pipes ran from one of the buildings to the enormous raised square of the launch pad.

A massive tower of scaffolding rose from the pad, high above the edge of the crater where the Doctor was standing. And braced against it by supporting struts, standing proud and defiant against the sky, was a huge rocket.

It was predominantly white, with black markings and 'USA' in huge letters down the side towards the bottom. Two-thirds of the way up, it tapered before continuing as the narrower cylinder that they had seen above the lip of the artificial crater.

'The Saturn Five,' Walinski said. 'Biggest launch vehicle ever built by Man. That one's serial number is SA-521, and it doesn't officially exist.'

'You said there were several secret Apollo missions to the moon, to set up Base Diana,' the Doctor remembered.

'That's right,' Candace answered. 'Apollo 18 to Apollo 22. Then they got the quantum displacement systems activated and working, so they didn't need the trouble and expense of another rocket.'

'But they already had one waiting,' Walinski said. 'Couldn't easily get rid of it without attracting attention and raising a few questions. The officially aborted Apollo 18 and 19 rockets, and the back-up Skylab launch vehicle were already decommissioned and on display at Houston, Kennedy, and the Space and Rockets Center at Hunsville, Alabama.'

'So this one stayed here,' Candace said. 'Notionally as an emergency back-up, ready to be fuelled for take-off at a week's notice.'

'Except that was thirty years ago,' Walinski told them. 'Who knows what condition she's really in now?'

'And we don't have a week,' the Doctor said. 'We have twenty-four hours at most to get her ready.' He clapped his hands together excitedly. 'And we'll need to speed up the journey too. Apollo 11 took four days to reach the moon. I want to be there in forty-eight hours.'

'This baby will be quicker than the first moonshots,' Candace said. 'They found a way to use the M3 Variant fuel developed by the British Rocket Group for their aborted Mars Probe Missions way back. That'll shave a lot off the journey time.'

The Doctor brandished his sonic screwdriver. 'And I can shave off even more.'

'You know,' Candace said, 'this is not sounding as crazy as I thought it would. If you'd told me yesterday that we'd be seriously considering getting that thing ready for launch, I'd have said you were mad. But somehow, now we're here, looking at her... Well, it sounds so plausible.'

'If that thing will actually work after all this time,'
Jennings said. 'And if you can find anyone experienced
enough and crazy enough to agree to fly it.'

'So we're looking for three astronauts,' Walinski
said.

'Two,' the Doctor told him. 'You've got me
already.'

'Like you're trained up for this sort of thing,'
Candace said.

'Got my Mars-Venus license,' the Doctor said,
apparently affronted. 'Probably better qualified than
anyone else you can rustle up. Ask Jennings here, he's
read the files.'

Jennings nodded. 'Don't ask,' he said. 'Just
believe.'

After a moment's silence, Candace said: 'Pat
Ashton is notionally in charge of keeping that thing
in shape. He's got experience on the shuttle, so he can
probably pilot it.'

'And Marty Garrett is back from his shopping trip,'
Jennings added. 'He has more hours as Technical
Officer on Base Diana than anyone. Be a good idea
to take him anyway to help sort out the problems
there.'

'Garrett's the astronaut who turned up at the
burger bar, yes?' the Doctor checked. 'Then I only
have one question before we start getting this thing
literally off the ground.'

'And what's that?' Walinski asked.

The Doctor nodded at the colossal rocket in front
of them. 'Does she have a name?'

Walinski laughed. 'She sure does, though it's not very imaginative. She may not officially exist, but you are now looking at Apollo 23.'

Chapter

15

With his automatic pistol in a shoulder holster under his uniform jacket, Captain Reeve led the way to Jackson's office.

'Not all aliens are afraid of guns,' Amy warned him.

Once again, Reeve surprised her by taking her statement seriously and not questioning how she might have come by this information. 'His body's human even if his mind is alien.'

'Fair enough. Let's hope he realises that.'

'We'll make sure he does.'

Jackson's door was closed. Amy half hoped he wasn't in his office. But they had already passed the empty Process Chamber. Next port of call would be Jackson's living quarters.

'Leave this to me, OK?' Reeve said, knocking on the door.

'You're the man with the gun. You can do the

talking.'

Jackson's voice was muffled by the door as he called for them to enter. He was working at his desk, and stood up as Reeve and Amy went in.

'Captain, Miss Pond. What a delightful surprise. What, may I ask, brings you to my humble abode? Do, please, clear a space and sit down. Can I get you some tea?' He gestured to the metal water heater nearby.

'We're not here to chat, Professor,' Reeve said shortly.

'Oh that's a pity. Then why are you here, may I ask?'

In answer, Reeve drew his gun. 'I'm afraid the game's up, Professor Jackson. Miss Pond has been doing a bit of investigating on her own account. She knows everything.'

Jackson raised an eyebrow. 'Everything? Oh I seriously doubt that.'

'You're not denying it then,' Amy said.

'I'm not quite sure yet what I'm being accused of, so no – I'm not denying anything at the moment.'

'Miss Pond has been to Pod 7,' Reeve said. 'She's seen what's inside. She knows that you've been downloading alien minds into the blank bodies created by your process.'

'Does she now?' Jackson looked thoughtful rather than anxious.

'Yes she does,' Amy told him, hoping to wipe the smugness from his tone and the half-smile from his face. 'So like Captain Reeve says, the game's up. You and Nurse Phillips and whoever else you've got control over will have to come quietly.'

Jackson sat down again. 'And what are you going to do with us, young lady? Shoot us?'

'No,' Amy told him. 'We're going to lock you in the empty cells in the prison hub. We'll keep you there until the Doctor comes back. He'll know what to do with you.'

'Except that the Doctor isn't coming back. How can he?'

'He'll find a way,' Amy said, sounding more confident than she felt. 'It's all over, Jackson. You're in a whole heap of trouble, and you know it.'

Jackson nodded slowly. 'I was right to accelerate the schedule and disable the quantum systems. Whoever sabotaged them originally did us a favour there. This is getting out of hand. The sooner we take over the whole of Base Diana and make preparations to infiltrate the minds of the people of Earth, the better.'

Amy gave a snort of derisive laughter. 'You just don't get it, do you? It's all over. The invasion's off. In case you hadn't noticed, Captain Reeve has a gun pointing at you.'

Jackson cleared his throat, a strangely apologetic sound. 'I'm afraid it's you that doesn't "get it", as you say, Miss Pond. In case you hadn't noticed, Captain Reeve's gun is not pointing at *me*.'

Amy felt the colour drain from her face. Slowly, she turned to look at Reeve. She already knew what she would see, even before Jackson added:

'The gun is pointing at *you*, Miss Pond.'

Above the pistol pointing straight at Amy's head,

Captain Reeve smiled. But his eyes were cold and grey as stone. 'I'm so sorry,' he said quietly. 'But I couldn't risk you telling anyone else what you'd found out. After all, you never know who you can trust these days, do you?'

'Apparently not.' Amy could have kicked herself. Then again, she thought, Reeve had found her in Pod 7. If she'd realised he was being controlled by the aliens, he'd still have brought her to Jackson. 'So what are you going to do to me? Put me through your process machinery?'

'Of course,' Jackson said in a matter-of-fact tone. 'But the schedule is very precise. We can only instil one of our minds into a human brain at certain predetermined times. The signals from our home world are timed to the second.' He smiled. 'But rest assured we are fixing that. Soon there will be a constant supply of thought and personality data that we can tap into and siphon off at will.'

'The next signal isn't due for a few hours yet,' Reeve said. 'I suggest we adopt Miss Pond's own plan and lock her in the hub until then.'

'There's a spare cell now that Nine is no longer with us,' Jackson agreed. 'Very well. I was going to start downloading into the Blanks in Pod 7, but we can wipe and replace in a single operation.'

'Sounds great,' Amy said sarcastically.

'I'm afraid not. There will be considerable pain.'

'You don't sound too upset about it.'

Jackson seemed surprised at the comment. 'Why would I be? It's not me who'll be feeling the pain.'

'Oh yes it is,' Amy said. 'Maybe not yet, but soon…

Trust me – you'll feel it.'

Jackson fixed his grey eyes on her, regarding Amy without expression.

'Take her away,' he said.

It seemed as though the base was deserted. Amy guessed that when the aliens had brought forward their plans, Reeve had consigned all the soldiers to their quarters, or made sure they were busy well away from Pod 7 and the cells.

Her only moment of hope on the way back to the central hub was when a uniformed figure appeared from a doorway ahead of them. Should she call for help? Would Reeve really shoot her, even with someone else there to witness it? It took her less than a moment to decide he would – he could explain it away. Blame her for the sabotage, or whatever. He might just shoot them both.

Or the soldier in front of them might already have been taken over. The figure turned and Amy saw that it was Major Carlisle. Her last glimmer of hope faded into dark despair.

'What's going on?' Carlisle demanded.

'I'm putting her in the cells,' Reeve said.

'Why?'

'Because I know,' Amy said. 'I know everything about your plan, about who you really are and what's going on here.'

Carlisle stared back at Amy, her expression giving nothing away.

'She's seen inside Pod 7,' Reeve said.

'Which is more than I have,' Carlisle retorted.

'But you've been processed. So you know what's in there.'

Carlisle blinked. 'Of course.' She drew her handgun. 'All right, Captain. I'll take her from here.'

'Thank you, Major,' Reeve said. 'But I want to see her in a cell myself.'

Carlisle glanced at Amy. 'Not surprised. All right, come on then.' She jabbed the handgun into Amy's ribs. 'Move it.'

Amy had about two seconds to grab the gun. She could do it – she *knew* she could. While Carlisle was staring into her face, almost daring her to try. But she couldn't move; she was frozen with sudden fear. What if the gun went off? What if Major Carlisle *wanted* her to try it?

Then the moment was lost. Almost reluctantly, it seemed to Amy, Carlisle withdrew the gun, and motioned for Amy to continue down the corridor.

As they approached the hub, Amy knew she had no chances left. There was no way back, and the only other escape route from the hub area was down the corridor to Pod 7. No way out.

Unless...

There was something stirring at the back of her memory. Something to do with the route to Pod 7 – think. *Think.*

It came to her as the door slid open and they entered the foyer area with its huge window looking out at the prison block at the hub of Base Diana. If she could just get to the far end of the long room, to the door to the corridor down to Pod 7.

Major Carlisle pushed her roughly forwards, as

if sensing that Amy was planning something. But if it was her intention to frighten Amy out of it, the action had the opposite effect. It gave Amy her one, last chance.

Surprised, Amy went staggering across the foyer. Behind her, Captain Reeve laughed. As she managed to catch her balance, Amy glared back at the two soldiers. Carlisle had stepped in front of Reeve as she followed Amy – blocking the Captain's gun. Carlisle's own gun was still in her hand, but her hand was by her side as she watched Amy. The Major smiled, as if pleased with her handiwork.

But to Amy it signalled that she could go for it – all or nothing. Now or never.

Do or die.

Still staggering backwards, she turned and kept going – running as fast as her long legs would take her down the long room.

'Stop her!' Reeve yelled.

'Oh don't worry,' Carlisle replied. 'Where can she go? What can she do?'

Amy knew exactly what she could do, if only she could get there. She didn't turn back as she heard Carlisle's shout of realisation:

'If she sets off the evacuation alarm, she'll open all the doors. She'll release the prisoners!'

She hadn't been sure *what* breaking the square glass plate would do. The most Amy had hoped for was a distraction – something that might bring help from soldiers not yet possessed by the aliens. But right now releasing the prisoners sounded like a good idea.

She jabbed at the glass plate with her crooked elbow, shattering it.

Immediately a klaxon started to sound. Red emergency lighting cut in, flashing in time with the noise of the alarm. The doors at either end of the foyer area slid open – and so did the doors all along it. The doors to the cells.

Captain Reeve was staring in horror at the opening doors, his gun raised. Major Carlisle looking along the length of the room at Amy. There was the ghost of a smile on her face, as if she knew already that Amy's action had been in vain.

Then the prisoners appeared in the doorways, and they were not what Amy had expected at all.

She wasn't sure what she *had* expected – large, fierce-looking men with broken noses and a wealth of tattoos maybe. Not thin, emaciated figures in ill-fitting overalls. Some of the men were barely out of their teens. There were women too, their faces haunted and eyes sunken. All of them looked half dead with exhaustion and despair.

If she had a moment of distraction, a moment to get past Reeve and Carlisle and escape, this was it. But Amy didn't take it. All she felt was horror and pity. It sapped her strength and she fell back against the wall, trembling.

'Oh you poor people,' she murmured. 'What have they done to you?'

Chapter

16

The Mission Control building at the Johnson Space Center in Houston had three main floors. The first two contained identical control rooms. The third floor was allocated to the US Department of Defense, and housed a mission control suite very similar to the others. Except that on the third floor there were no cameras, no press access, no way for details of military-funded space projects to leave the room.

It was impossible for any other agency – even NASA itself – to get access to this floor, let alone 'borrow' it to control a secret launch of their own. It took Agent Jennings eleven minutes to get agreement from the Joint Chiefs of Staff.

Candace Hecker personally chose the control staff. Flight Controller was Daniel Bardell, veteran of a dozen shuttle launches. Jennings, Hecker and Walinski watched from the back of the room as Bardell checked each of his senior technicians was happy.

'I need a *Go* or *No-Go* decision from each of you.'

'I'm getting some seriously weird readings here from one of the crew,' the Medical Officer called.

The Doctor's voice came over the speakers loud and clear: 'Ignore that. Otherwise all right?'

Bardell nodded his agreement to the medical officer.

'I guess. That's a Go, then, Flight.'

It was incredible, Candace thought, that just twenty-four hours earlier no one had really believed the huge Saturn V would ever leave the ground. Now it was fuelled and ready, waiting in the secret crater several hundred miles away in the vast, empty desert. The crew was installed in the Command Module – a tiny capsule at the top of the enormous structure. The Doctor's non-stop, frenetic work leading a team of technicians had achieved the impossible.

'Go, Flight,' confirmed the last of the technicians.

'Then let's get this baby off the ground,' Bardell said. 'We are at T-minus 40... 39... 38...'

Jennings leaned over to Candace, and asked quietly: 'You seriously think this is going to work?'

'The Doctor does.'

'You really respect that guy, don't you?'

Candace nodded. 'I've seen him working the last day. Never mind six impossible things before breakfast, he'll get through sixty and still have time to make the toast.'

'He knows how to get the best out of other people, too,' Walinski put in. 'He inspires them. His enthusiasm rubs off.' The General turned back to face the main screen at the front of the room. As well as numerous data feeds and graphs, it showed a live video feed of the huge rocket, smoke drifting from beneath it.

Overlaid on this main image was the countdown: 19... 18... 17...

'Guidance release,' a technician announced.

15... 14... 13... 12... 11... 10...

'Main engine start.'

Fire and smoke erupted from the bottom of the rocket. It trembled on the launch pad.

'All Stage One engines, thrust OK.'

The metal gantries from the launch tower to the side of the rocket swung clear. Cables dropped away.

'Umbilical disconnected.'

Slowly, almost ponderously, the Saturn V began to lift. At first it seemed like it would rise only inches from the pad on its cushion of smoke and flame.

'We have lift-off.'

Then it gathered speed. A cascade of ice crumbled from the sides of the rocket, so cold from the liquefied fuel inside, and fell in chunks into the roaring flames spewing from the engines. The rocket continued to rise.

'Apollo 23 has cleared the tower,' a technician declared as the engines passed over the scaffolding structure that had supported the rocket.

Less than a minute later, the spacecraft reached the speed of sound. A minute and a half after that, all fuel exhausted, the first stage dropped away and the second stage rockets fired, powering Apollo 23 onwards.

There was a smattering of applause in the control

room. Candace Hecker couldn't suppress a grin. She was pleased to see that Walinski and Jennings were both smiling too.

'Well done,' Walinski told her.

'That's the easy part over,' Jennings joked. 'Now it's up to the Doctor.'

Candace checked her watch. 'With the adapted M3 Variant fuel and the modifications the Doctor made, they should achieve lunar orbit in about eighteen hours. They'll land as soon as they can after that.'

'So long as nothing goes wrong,' Jennings said.

'You're a pessimist,' Walinski told him.

'I'm a realist,' Jennings countered. 'If the Doctor's right and there's an alien invasion force gathering up there, how much do you want to bet they know he's coming?'

'But what can they do?' Candace asked.

'I guess we'll find out,' Jennings said quietly.

A voice rang out from the speakers. A single word from the most experienced of the crew of Apollo 23 as they began their journey: 'Geronimo!'

Several hours out from lunar orbit, the third stage of the Saturn V disengaged to reveal the pod where the Lunar Excursion Module was stored. The tiny Service Module with the main capsule – the Command Module – attached to it swung round to dock with the LEM, the craft that would actually land on the moon's surface.

All that now remained of the huge craft that had taken off from the Texan desert was a stubby cylinder with a single rocket engine, attached nose-first to a fragile module made largely out of thick metal foil. With its four landing legs folded underneath itself, the LEM looked like a glittering spider ready to pounce.

'You reckon they know you're coming?' Pat Ashton asked.

The three astronauts were making the final checks before entering lunar orbit. The Doctor was in the middle of the three chairs, Pat Ashton on one side and Marty Garrett on the other. Ashton was the Command Module pilot – he would stay in orbit while the Doctor and Garrett descended to the moon in the LEM.

'Oh they know,' the Doctor said without turning from the controls he was checking. 'They'll have seen us coming.'

'Base Diana might be on the dark side of the moon,' Garrett said, 'but there are satellites to bounce radio signals down to them. They'll have tracked us most of the way.' He grinned. 'Probably wondering who we are and what we're doing.'

'They'll be waiting for you, then,' Ashton said. 'You ready for that?'

'I'm ready for anything,' the Doctor told him. 'Question is – are they ready for me?'

'You got some experience of tackling alien invaders then?' Garrett asked. His tone was suddenly serious. His eyes seemed to lose colour as he turned slightly to watch the Doctor answer.

'Just a bit. Well, quite a lot actually.' The Doctor adjusted a dial and tapped a gauge. 'That's funny.' He glanced at Garrett. 'Don't worry, we'll be fine. I don't expect they'll give me much trouble.'

Ashton leaned forward to examine the same dial as the Doctor had tapped, straining against the straps holding him into his seat. 'Looks like a radio wave,' he muttered. 'But there's nothing on the speakers. Nothing from Houston.'

'There wouldn't be,' the Doctor said. 'That's coming from the opposite direction.' He pointed a gloved hand towards another readout. 'See? A signal of some sort. But what's it for?'

'It's for me,' Garrett replied, his voice devoid of expression. A moment later, his booted foot slammed into the centre of the control console.

Sparks erupted from shattered dials and gauges. A mass of red indicator lights blazed into life. A buzzer sounded insistently. Garrett drew his foot back, ready to kick out again. The whole ship lurched, throwing him sideways in his seat. His colourless grey eyes glared across at the Doctor, who was already unstrapping and floating clear of his seat.

'What the hell?' Ashton yelled above the alarms and the explosions. 'Are you crazy?!'

'Possessed more like,' the Doctor yelled back. 'Get this thing under control.'

Ashton struggled with his straps, floating clear of his seat to grab a small fire extinguisher.

Garrett was also free, kicking against a bulkhead to float after the Doctor. There was no escape in the tiny cabin.

'What's going on up there?' Bardell's voice was tinny and distorted by the speakers. 'We've got alarms going like crazy down here. You guys OK?'

'Not now,' Ashton shouted back, 'We've got problems.'

Garrett was holding a heavy metal spanner. He swung it at the Doctor, who managed to roll backwards out of the way. The movement spun Garrett too, disorientating him as he turned lazily in the zero gravity.

'I'll get him out of your way,' the Doctor shouted to Ashton. 'It's me he's after.'

'There's nowhere to go!' Ashton pointed out. But his voice was lost as another alarm went off. Ashton punched the button to reset it. 'We're venting fuel. That's not good.' He glanced round as he worked, wondering what he could do to help the Doctor – wondering what had happened to Garrett.

But the capsule behind him was empty.

The docking linkway between the Command Module and the LEM was only a few metres long. The Doctor launched himself through the hatch from the main capsule, glancing back to check that Garrett was following him. With luck, Ashton would be able to sort out the problems caused by Garrett's foot… If not, then it didn't really matter if the Doctor could escape Garrett or not – they'd all be dead.

If he'd had time and thought about it, the Doctor would have brought his helmet. Without that, it didn't matter that he was wearing his spacesuit. The Apollo craft was so fragile – designed to be as light as possible, not to endure an attack from a possessed man. What had Amy said they were called? Blanks.

That made sense. The radio signal, the transmission

was a download of some sort – instructions beamed into Garrett's mind. The man's eyes were pale grey as he floated down the linkway after the Doctor. As if the humanity had been drained out of him as well as the colour.

'When did they get you?' the Doctor asked.

Garrett didn't answer. No chance in engaging him in conversation while the Doctor thought of a plan, then.

'Not in your instructions to answer, I suppose.' The Doctor pushed off gently from a control console in the LEM, floating across the small craft. Garrett had to change course to follow him, flailing for a while in the weightless environment before he could adjust.

'Is it a switch, in the true sense of the word?' the Doctor wondered out loud. 'Your mind primed and ready to be switched off, changed for a new set of instructions? Presumably instructions to ensure that I don't make it back to the moon.'

Garrett was braced against the opposite side of the LEM, ready to launch himself at the Doctor.

'Maybe you had to gauge if I was a threat first. Hence the questions about my experience with alien invaders.'

In a blur of motion that defied the graceful, weightlessness the Doctor was experiencing, Garrett flew across the LEM. His hand snatched at the Doctor.

But the Doctor was already pushing himself away, out of reach. 'Maybe that's why you ended up on Earth. Someone realised you'd been got at and sent you for a burger...' He remembered Amy recounting her story over the radio. 'Aha! Liz Didbrook, at a guess. The original saboteur, trying to attract attention when she realised something was terribly wrong on the moonbase. Then I guess Jackson realised that breaking the quantum link wasn't such a bad idea after all, so he could work in peace.'

Again, Garrett's sudden movement was a fraction of a second too slow. He crashed into a bulkhead. The whole craft shuddered. The Doctor could see the metal skin of the LEM shimmer close by as it stretched under the impact.

'I guess – that is, I *hope* – you're more used to the shuttle,' the Doctor said. 'If you remember anything of your own experience.' He'd managed to manoeuvre himself closer to the linkway back to the Command Module. He'd need to get out of here fast and close the door.

Garrett's blank face twitched in what might have been the hint of a smile.

'You think that if I shut the hatch, you can just open it again from this side,' the Doctor said. 'And you're right. There's no way to lock it. Except, to open it again you'd have to be still inside the LEM.'

The Doctor moved as he was speaking, pushing against the solid bulk of a storage locker. Immediately, Garrett hurled himself after the Doctor. He kicked out strongly against the wall behind him with both feet at once.

'They had to keep the weight right down, you know. And the walls in here are so light, so fragile, they're like tin foil,' the Doctor said.

But his words were lost in the sudden explosion of

167

noise as Garrett's feet kicked through the thin metal membrane of the LEM. The fragile skin was all that protected the occupants of the craft from the freezing vacuum of space.

Explosive decompression. The spaceship slammed sideways as the air was sucked out. Garrett's face was suddenly a mask of surprise, pain, and fear. For a fraction of a moment, his eyes were pale blue, staring back at the Doctor. Then he was gone – tumbling away into the vast blackness of space.

The Doctor braced himself against the wall of the linkway. Once he moved the hatch slightly, the air rushing past him slammed it shut. The Doctor spun the locking wheel.

'Turn the oxygen pumps off in the LEM,' the Doctor gasped. 'Otherwise it'll tear itself apart as the air escapes.'

Ashton battled to stabilise the capsule as it bucked and twisted, rolled and shook. Finally, the craft settled down and Ashton turned in his seat.

'Where's Garrett?'

The Doctor was looking through one of the thick triangular windows, sadly watching a tiny figure spinning away into the inky distance.

'He went outside,' the Doctor said. 'He might be quite some time.'

A cloud of fine grey dust kicked up from the main motor of the Lunar Module's descent stage. The wide pads settled into the lunar landscape. The dust floated gently down to the ground and everything was still again.

The hatchway opened. A figure in a red spacesuit clambered down the ladder. It bounced experimentally on its feet in the dusty surface. It mimed licking its finger through the spherical helmet and holding it up to check the non-existent wind.

'This way, I think,' the Doctor said, though he knew no one could hear him.

He blew upwards from the side of his mouth in an effort to detach a loose clump of hair that had flopped into his eyes. Maybe he needed one of those balaclava-like things that Garrett and Reeve and the others had worn under their helmets. Or maybe he could just stand on his head. He bounced again in the low gravity. Maybe not.

The Doctor glanced back at the LEM as he walked away from it. There was a dark gash down one side of it. The Doctor had done his best to patch the hole, for neatness as much as anything. In their full spacesuits, he and Ashton had pumped the air out of the Command Module before the Doctor had entered the LEM for the descent. The Doctor looked up, wondering if he'd catch a glimpse of Ashton going overhead. But the orbit would take a while yet. As soon as he was back on the right side of the moon, Ashton would report to Houston and Hibiscus. Now the Doctor was on his own.

Reaching the top of a shallow rise, the Doctor saw Base Diana lying in its shallow crater, almost exactly where he had expected to find it. He made no attempt to stay hidden – they knew he was coming. He strode down the incline towards the base, stuffing his hands absent-mindedly into pockets his spacesuit didn't have.

Whether they were waiting for him or not, the main airlock was a bit obvious. There must be another way in. The Doctor walked slowly round the base, expecting any moment to see white-spacesuited figures coming after him. But he saw no one. Not until he spotted Amy.

He caught sight of her hair first – a splash of colour against the white and grey. She was watching from a round porthole. The Doctor waved, and she waved back, then pointed to one side – the way she wanted him to go. The Doctor gave a clumsy thumbs-up hampered by his bulky glove, and followed her directions. Sure enough, a short way along was a small airlock. He pressed the access panel, and the door swung slowly open. The Doctor kept his helmet on, even though he could hear the air rushing in. Best to be careful. He might need to step outside again in a hurry.

But when the inner door opened, there was only Amy. She hugged him, struggling to get her arms round the large spacesuit. The Doctor removed his helmet and finally brushed the hair from his eyes.

'Been itching to do that for ages,' he told her. 'So what have you been up to, Pond – having fun?'

'We have to get away from here,' Amy said. 'They'll have seen you, or detected the airlock opening or something. We can't trust anyone, not any more. Jackson's accelerated the process. You know about the process?'

'Whoa, slow down.' The Doctor stripped off his spacesuit, adjusted his bow tie and straightened his crumpled jacket. 'Yes, I know about Jackson's process. And I'm fine thanks, pleased to see you too. Met some people, mended their rocket, fought off an alien assassin and here I am.'

'Good for you.' She didn't sound impressed. 'Come on, they've been after me for hours.'

Amy led the way through the base. Before long they reached the canteen. Amy glanced inside, then stepped back to let the Doctor see. The place was a mess – broken crockery strewn across the floor. Star-shaped patterns of dust and fragments where plates and bowls had broken apart.

'You'd think they'd have cleared it up,' Amy said.

'What happened?'

'Riot. I let the prisoners out. Got away from the bad guys in the confusion while the prisoners went on the rampage.'

The Doctor crouched down to examine the remains of a plate.

'They were throwing stuff,' Amy explained. 'But the soldiers rounded them up. Plates and cups against guns – no contest really.'

The Doctor straightened up, dusting his hands down his lapels. 'And you? What – you ran and hid?'

'Of course. I've been hiding for *days*. What else could I do?'

The Doctor nodded. He looked into her eyes and smiled sadly. 'What else could you do?' he agreed.

'So, what's the plan? How do we stop the Talerians now you're back?'

'Talerians?'

'That's what they call themselves. I overheard.'

'Interesting.' The Doctor drummed his fingers together. 'Yes, that makes sense. Um, plan – yes, right. Well we need to get to a transmitter. The radio we spoke on when I was stuck on Earth, that'll do.'

'Then what?'

The Doctor pulled out his sonic screwdriver. 'Then I can adjust the frequency, boost the signal, and send a jamming wave so no more Talerians can come through. Dealing with the ones already here will be easy enough. They'll be trapped so we can blow up the base and kill the lot of them.'

He paused, waiting to see if Amy reacted. But she said nothing.

'So they'll all die horribly, and serve them right,' he added. 'OK?'

'Fine. Sounds good to me.' Amy turned to go.

'I was afraid it might,' the Doctor murmured as he followed her down the corridor.

He soon recognised the section they were in, and was pleased if slightly surprised that they were close to the Communications Room.

'I sort of assumed the main computer systems would be somewhere near here,' the Doctor said. 'Makes sense to keep them together.'

'The processors, maybe,' Amy said. 'But not the data storage. That's all oxygenated hydrogen molecules. The spin of the electrons equates to the binary ones and zeroes. It's very cheap and highly efficient. Or so they tell me.'

'But a bit fragile and rather bulky,' the Doctor said. 'I suppose water hasn't been an issue till now though, so it makes sense. Cutting-edge stuff for this day and age. I didn't realise you were an expert.'

Amy paused in mid-step. 'Captain Reeve was telling me about it.'

'I see, I see,' the Doctor said casually, like it wasn't really important. In the same tone he went on: 'You're not really taking me to the Communications Room, are you?'

'No,' Amy said at once. She stopped. 'Ah. No...' She frowned. 'I had a better idea.'

'Thought so. I could tell. Written all over your face. I could see it in your eyes.' The Doctor had his sonic screwdriver out again. 'Your expressionless face. Your cold, grey eyes that are usually so bright and intelligent. So caring, but you didn't even blink when I said I'd kill the aliens and not even try to save the people they've mind-wiped. And then there's the crockery in the canteen.'

'What?' Amy was still, face blank as the Doctor shone his screwdriver in her eyes.

'It hadn't been thrown at anyone. You can tell by the pattern it made when it broke. Those plates were dropped. Your Talerian masters like to put on a bit of a show, do they?'

Her voice was completely level. 'I don't know what you mean.'

'If that's true, it's only because you've not been programmed with the information. But you're up to date on the local data storage, so that must be important. A race that can download itself into people's brains must be conscientious enough to keep back-ups after all.' The Doctor stepped closer, adjusting the settings on the sonic screwdriver. 'Now then, where are you, Amy? Are you still in there somewhere? They must be using some sort of alpha-wave inhibitor to suppress the host personality...'

From behind him, the Doctor heard the sound of someone clapping. Amy's eyes closed and her head tilted forwards, as if she was falling asleep. The Doctor turned slowly round.

Professor Jackson and Captain Reeve were standing behind him. Reeve was holding a gun. Hurrying to join them was Major Carlisle, her face as blank and expressionless as Amy's had been.

'Shame.' The Doctor pocketed his screwdriver. 'Thought I'd have more time than that.'

'Time to carry out your ridiculous plan to jam our signals?' Jackson sneered.

'Oh, that wasn't my plan,' the Doctor told him. 'Made that up for Amy when I saw she was under the influence.' He grinned widely. 'I've got a different ridiculous plan to defeat you.'

'Well, whatever it is, it's over,' Reeve snapped.

'And what about Amy – is she over?'

'Her program came to an end when we arrived,' Jackson said. 'The Blank can follow a simple set of instructions, then afterwards it is again simply... Blank.'

The Doctor took a step forwards, but Reeve jabbed his gun in warning. 'If you've hurt her...'

Jackson laughed. 'Empty threats, Doctor. You know, the hardest part was programming in enough information so that she could cope with any questions you might have – about us, Base Diana, anything. But when it comes down to it, you're not so impressive after all. We needn't have bothered.'

'But then I wouldn't know that you're really Talerians.'

'Which probably means nothing to you,' Reeve said.

The Doctor shrugged. 'So where is Amy? What have you done with her mind, her essence, her personality?'

'We've wiped it,' Jackson said simply. 'It's gone. For ever. And soon, your mind will follow. The next transmission is due in an hour. You will be blanked, and then imprinted with a new personality – with one of us.'

The Doctor nodded. 'What a surprise. But that still gives me an hour. An hour for you to tell me all about who you are, what you're up to, why you've decided to invade Earth. An hour for a chat and cup of tea – what do you say?'

'I say, an hour for you to ponder your fate and see what your meddling has done to your friend. An hour in a cell in the prison hub while I prepare the Process Chamber.' Jackson smiled, but the expression did not reach his cold, grey eyes. 'This time, Doctor, there really is no escape.'

Chapter

18

The gun jabbed painfully in the Doctor's ribs.

'I'm going to enjoy locking you up to await your fate,' Captain Reeve said. 'Just as I enjoyed locking up your friend.'

'I'm sure,' the Doctor said.

Jackson was already striding off down the corridor. 'I'll need some help,' he called back.

'You go,' Major Carlisle told Reeve, unholstering her own pistol. Her mouth twisted into a vicious smile. 'I'll deal with these two. My turn to have fun.'

Reeve stared back at her for a moment. Then he nodded. 'I'll see you again soon, Doctor. And I shall watch every moment of the process with interest.'

'Bye then,' the Doctor said. 'See you later.'

Reeve's face showed a flicker of amusement at the Doctor's apparent indifference. Then he turned on his heel and marched off down the corridor after Jackson.

Carlisle turned back to the Doctor and Amy. Her gun was aimed unerringly at the Doctor.

'Funny how some life forms can be so clever and yet miss the obvious,' the Doctor said. 'Mind you, humans are the same.'

'What do you mean?' Carlisle demanded.

The Doctor leaned towards her. He tapped the side of his nose conspiratorially. 'I mean,' he said, 'that your eyes are the wrong colour. They're chocolate brown, and if you're really a Talerian, they should be grey like Jackson's and Reeve's. And Amy's.'

Major Carlisle's smile was more genuine now. She glanced over her shoulder, checking that Jackson and Reeve had gone. 'Perhaps they're colour blind. They did actually process me, so they have an excuse.'

'What went wrong?'

Carlisle shrugged. 'Power failure at a critical point, I think. It's all a bit muzzy, to be honest. I can sort of hear one of them, like it's trapped in my head. So I've got some clues as to how to play along. But I'm hoping you can fill in the blanks.'

'That's what I'm here for.' The Doctor took Amy's lifeless hand, feeling for her faint pulse. 'Literally to fill in the Blanks. With their own personalities again.'

'I tried to help her,' Carlisle said as the Doctor inspected Amy's eyes. 'I gave her a chance to grab my gun, but I think she was too scared. Then I helped her let the prisoners out.'

'Was there really a riot?' the Doctor wondered. 'Amy said that was how she escaped. Except of course she didn't.'

Carlisle shook her head. 'The prisoners are in no

state to cause trouble. A distraction, no more. She could have made a run for it, but she... Well, I guess she was just shocked. She seemed to want to help them.'

'That sounds like Amy.'

'Reeve got her. They blanked her out, or whatever, and here we are. Is there anything you can do for her? For any of them? I don't know Jackson, not really, but Jim Reeve was a good man.'

'Let's hope he still is,' the Doctor said. 'And that we can find where they've stored him.'

'Stored him? What do you mean?'

'I mean they kept a back-up copy of his personality. At least, I'm hoping they did.'

All the time they had been talking, the Doctor had been examining Amy – checking her pulse, her eyes, looking for any sign of self-will or consciousness. There was nothing.

'So what's the plan?' Carlisle said.

'Amy asked me that.' The Doctor turned and looked into the Major's eyes. 'Double bluff? No, I don't think so.' Suddenly, he reached out and grabbed her hand, including the gun. But he wasn't trying to get the gun from her, he shook her hand – gun and all. 'Welcome to the team. And the team plan is to get to the main computer facility. You know where that is?'

Carlisle nodded, still startled by the Doctor's sudden handshake. 'What do we do with your friend?'

'She can come with us.' The Doctor waved his sonic screwdriver. 'Quick bit of optical stimulation and she'll respond to simple verbal instructions. I hope.'

'Quick bit of what?'

'I'm going to shine a light in her eyes.'

Access to the computer facility was on the other side of the base. But with the Doctor and Amy accompanied by Major Carlisle, there was a chance they could make it without being challenged. If they were, Carlisle had her gun – either to bluff she was taking her prisoners to the hub, or for defence.

'There are only a few of the guys left who haven't been processed,' Carlisle explained. 'A lot of the others don't even know they've been blanked. They're programmed to act as normal until they're ordered otherwise. Means we have no idea who we can trust. But I guess that bears out your theory they're keeping the original personalities on file somewhere. Somehow.'

'I guess it does,' the Doctor agreed. 'They'd need to reload the original personality data temporarily, with an instruction to blank it out or override it when necessary.'

He stopped at a junction of two corridors. Behind him, Amy kept walking, silent and blank-faced, and cannoned into the back of him.

'Yeah, right, when I said to follow me I kind of meant "and stop when I stop" sort of thing, right?'

She didn't answer, but stood waiting for the Doctor and Carlisle to move on.

'She's very literal-minded,' Carlisle said.

'Not usually.' The Doctor sighed. 'Someone is going to be in *so* much trouble for this,' he said quietly. 'Right – onwards!'

They passed a couple of soldiers, who acknowledged Major Carlisle, but didn't seem concerned or worried by the fact she was with the Doctor and Amy. Carlisle kept her gun out of sight, but ready in case she needed it.

Gradually, as they moved along, the base seemed less utilised. There was dust on the floor, and the lighting was at a lower level.

'No one comes here much,' Carlisle explained. 'Just for maintenance. Like the quantum displacement equipment, the computer facility is in the basement, built into the bedrock under the crater. For good reason.'

'Oh? What reason is that, then?' the Doctor asked her.

Before she could reply, a white-coated man stepped out of a side corridor just in front of them. He stared in surprise at the Doctor and Amy, then looked enquiringly at Carlisle.

'What are you doing here? Professor Jackson's put this whole area off limits, except for his personal assistants.'

'I know that, Gregman,' Carlisle snapped. Her hand edged towards her gun.

But Gregman was quicker. He pulled a pistol from his pocket and aimed it at the Doctor. 'I shall have to report this. You'd better have a very good reason for being here. The Doctor is meant to be in a cell awaiting his turn in the Process Chamber. I know, because Professor Jackson sent me to connect a back-up unit ready for the transfer.'

'Ah, so you do keep back-ups,' the Doctor said.

'That's good to know. It means we're heading the right way.'

'Not any longer.' Gregman jabbed the gun towards Carlisle. 'Keep your sidearm holstered, Major,' he warned.

Carlisle raised her hands to show she had no intention of going for her gun. As she did so, a figure pushed past her. She assumed it was the Doctor, but it wasn't. It was Amy.

Blank-faced, she walked slowly towards Gregman. He frowned, watching her. 'You can stop now,' he said. 'Your programming is at an end. Just blank out. Stop.'

But she kept walking, past Gregman and on down the corridor. Confused, the scientist turned, tracking her with the gun.

'I said stop! Stop, or I'll—'

His words became a grunt of surprise and pain as the butt of Carlisle's gun thumped into the back of his head. Gregman collapsed to the floor, and Carlisle stood over the unconscious man, gun aimed.

'Just leave him,' the Doctor said, striding past.

'But—'

'If you shoot him, we can never return the real Gregman's mind to his body,' the Doctor pointed out. 'Now stop dithering, and come on.'

He turned down the side corridor from which Gregman had come. 'This way, Amy.'

'She'd stopped,' Carlisle said as she followed the Doctor. 'She'd stopped, like you told her to when we did. Then she started walking again and distracted Gregman. Was that deliberate? Can she have done it on purpose, do you think?'

They both paused, waiting for Amy to catch up with them. She shuffled along like a sleepwalker, eyes wide and staring – unseeing.

'Possibly,' the Doctor said. 'If they don't completely remove the original personality, then perhaps something's still in there somewhere. Deep down, waiting for something to latch on to. Desperate to reassert itself. An instinct, a spark in the darkness. A little touch of Amy in the night.'

They reached a security door. Carlisle keyed in her code and the door swung open.

'At least they haven't recoded it.'

The Doctor aimed his sonic screwdriver at the keypad. 'No, but I have. Reset it to the factory settings, they'll never guess. The code is now 1234.'

Beyond the door, a metal stairway descended into darkness. From below they could hear a constant drip-drip of water. It was like descending into a cave system – the metal walls of the base soon gave way to dark rock, glistening with condensation.

'Vacuum-sealed to save having to clad the whole place in airtight panels,' the Doctor said.

He started down the stairs, his feet echoing on the steps. Carlisle followed, with Amy close behind. The door swung shut with an ominous clang, leaving them in near darkness.

'It's like descending into the depths of hell itself,' the Doctor said.

'Oh and you'd know what that's like, would you?' Carlisle retorted. Her voice was strained and nervous and she followed the Doctor.

He paused to look back up at her. His face was shadowed and grave. 'Do I really need to answer that?'

Carlisle shivered. There was something in the way he said it that told her she didn't want to know about some of the places he had been. And hell could very well be one of them. With Amy close behind her, she followed the Doctor down into the depths below Base Diana.

Chapter

19

A glimmer of light from far below was their only illumination. It grew slowly but steadily as the Doctor, Carlisle and Amy made their way down the stairs. They seemed to descend for ever, into the depths of the moon. The walls glistened and sweated.

'They must pump the water through using the quantum displacement system,' the Doctor said.

'No, it was here already,' Carlisle told him.

'Really?'

'A huge underground lake. You may have heard that NASA found minute quantities of water on the moon. No one was meant to know anything at all about it, but news got out.'

'You mean there was a leak?' The Doctor grinned. Carlisle didn't seem to appreciate the joke. The Doctor cleared his throat and went on: 'So there's actually quite a bit of water here. That's a surprise. Isn't it?' He looked confused for a moment, then his face cleared.

'Yes, must be. Just checking.'

'Base Diana was positioned right on top of the water. Seemed stupid not to make use of the natural resources.'

The Doctor ran his finger down the damp rock wall, then licked it. 'Sustenance, hygiene, and computer storage with data held in the H_2O molecules. What more does anyone need?'

At the bottom of the steps, they found themselves in a vast underground cavern. Banks of computer equipment stretched off into the distance. Fluorescent light strips cast puddles of stark light between the aisles of machinery. Huge metal pipes were visible at the far end of the cavern, bringing in water from the reservoir. Transparent tubes ran between the banks of equipment, carrying water – and the data it held within its molecules, round the systems. Carlisle could see tiny bubbles of air being carried along, indicating the end of one parcel of data and the start of another.

The Doctor clapped his hands together, delighted and impressed, and hurried over to a console.

'Most of this is storage,' he explained. 'Data streaming – literally. Great stuff!'

The screen lit up and the Doctor rattled away at a keyboard. He displayed a schematic of the reservoir and water system. It showed where the water was purified and then held in various tanks to service the drinking supply and bathrooms as well as the data storage.

'The water is electrolysed here, before being pumped into the computer systems as needed,' the

Doctor said, pointing to a point on the plan where water entered the cavern. 'Light would be a quicker medium, but they were after efficiency and durability rather than speed, plus the water cools the systems as well. Brilliant. Conventional systems with hard drives and flash memory for the day-to-day tasks, and everything offloaded and backed-up to the hydrogen dioxide for the longer term.'

'So how does that help?' Carlisle wondered.

'We've got Amy's physical body.' The Doctor turned and nodded at his expressionless friend standing silent and immobile beside them. 'Now we need to find her brain. She shouldn't be just a pretty face, you know.'

'Goes without saying,' Carlisle told him.

'What's this?' The Doctor was pointing to another tank. 'It's connected into the reservoir system, but there's a flow valve keeping it isolated.'

'Looks like the inert gas for the fire suppression systems. Worst-case scenario – if we run out of the gas before the fire's out, then the valve opens and it draws in water. Not ideal, given we're so dependent on electrical stuff.'

'But could be the only option, the last resort.' The Doctor nodded. 'Makes sense. Whoever designed this place used belts and braces all round.'

'Is that how you got back here?' Carlisle asked.

'I suppose so. Big braces though. Enormous. Right...' He turned his attention back to the display screen and started opening files of indexes and data listings. 'Let's find Amy...'

*

For the briefest of moments, he thought he was Lars Gregman. Then the Talerian consciousness flowed back into the emptiness of Gregman's mind and he remembered everything.

Gregman sat up. There was pain in his head. Not the pain of the process when he had been transferred into this body. It was reassuringly robust, but it could be damaged. He reached his hand behind his head and felt the lump where Carlisle had struck him down.

Carlisle. For some reason she was helping the Doctor. The girl, Amy, was a Blank – no use to them. Perhaps even a weapon against them if she could be reprogrammed…

Struggling to his feet, Gregman looked round. He had no idea how long he had been unconscious, but he was surprised and pleased to find his gun was lying a short distance away. He knew where the Doctor and Carlisle were headed – he could deal with them himself. It would impress Jackson.

Except that when he tapped in the code for the door down to the computer facility, it didn't work. The door remained locked. But even this was a good thing, he decided. It meant they were definitely down there. There was nothing the Doctor or Major Carlisle could do to stop the Talerian plan now. Soon the main invasion force would come through, and the only person they feared might be able to stop them was trapped in the cavern under the base.

Gregman hurried to tell Jackson and the others the good news.

*

It didn't take the Doctor long to find what he was looking for. 'I'll say this for them, they're efficient.'

He showed Carlisle the screen, which displayed a list of the personnel of Base Diana. Against almost all of them was a catalogue number. At the bottom of the list was:

```
Amy Pond - E-19-K3
```

Below that were several other names, listed as 'Pending'. At the bottom of this pending list was 'Doctor'.

'What's it mean?' Major Carlisle asked.

'It means we've found her. You're on the list too, look.' He pointed to Carlisle's name.

'Doesn't mean I'm a bad person.'

'All the others are. Potentially, anyway. Until we get this sorted.'

The Doctor walked slowly along one of the aisles. Carlisle and Amy followed – Carlisle watching with interest, Amy expressionless.

The storage was rather like metal filing cabinets. Each aisle was labelled with a letter, and each cabinet within each aisle was numbered. The individual drawers bore letters, marked in black by a simple steel handle.

'This is aisle E, so I guess we're looking for storage cabinet 19,' Carlisle said.

'Drawer K.' The Doctor ran his finger down the front of Cabinet 19 until it met the K. He tapped the letter. 'Moment of truth. Who lives here, do you think?'

The Doctor pulled out the shallow drawer. Inside the space was lined with dark foam padding. Nestling in numbered compartments cut into the foam were ten glass phials filled with colourless liquid. A wire connected the stopper of each phial into a junction box at the back of the drawer.

Very carefully, the Doctor lifted phial 3 clear of the padding. The wire trailed from a small clip attached to the top of the stopper. Inside the phial another wire hung down into the liquid. The Doctor unclipped the wire from the top and lifted the phial up to the light. He gave it a gentle shake, bubbles rising to the surface.

'Is that it?' Carlisle asked in a whisper. She pointed at Amy. 'Is that... *her*?'

The Doctor stared intently at the colourless liquid. 'Amy in a bottle,' he breathed. 'Pond water.' He laughed. 'Yes, I like that. Pond water.' His smile faded. 'Only problem is, now I've found you, we need to get you both back to the Process Chamber and see if we can download the real you into your brain.'

From above and behind them came the sound of something heavy slamming into metal.

'The door?' Carlisle said.

'The door,' the Doctor agreed. 'They've found us.'

'Gregman must have woken up. Getting to the Process Chamber might be trickier than you thought.'

'No problem. We'll take the back way.' The Doctor clicked his tongue. 'Er, is there a back way?'

'No.'

'Any way at all, back or otherwise? Emergency

exit? Fire escape? Cat flap?'

Carlisle was shaking her head. 'There's only one exit, Doctor. We're stuck down here.' The sound of the banging was getting louder and more insistent. 'And that door won't keep them out for long.'

Chapter
20

The sound of the door crashing open was unmistakable. The Doctor spun round on the spot, slapping his forehead repeatedly with the heel of his hand.

'Think think think,' he told himself. 'Ah!' He stopped his rapid revolutions. 'They don't know we're down here.'

'Yes they do,' Carlisle said. 'Gregman knew we were heading this way.'

'And the door was locked and sabotaged. But they don't *know*, not for sure. They just think they do.'

Carlisle nodded slowly. 'Makes sense. But they'll be down those stairs in a minute, and then they'll know they know.'

The Doctor leaned forward. 'No they won't. Because I've got a plan.'

'Quick plan?'

They could hear feet on the metal stairway.

'Very quick.'

'So – what do we do?'

'We keep Amy safe.' The Doctor pushed the phial of liquid that was Amy's personality and memories into his top pocket and patted it gently.

'Is that it?' Carlisle asked.

'No no no. The clever bit is…'

'Yes?'

'… We hide.'

Carlisle stared at him. 'Is that it? The great plan? We *hide*?!'

The Doctor shrugged and flicked his hair out of his eyes. 'Unless you've got a better plan. One that doesn't involve shooting anyone,' he added. 'I want everyone's body intact so we can put their brains back where they're supposed to be.'

Carlisle glanced back towards the stairs. 'We hide,' she said.

The Doctor and Major Carlisle hurried quietly down the aisle. The cavern was vast and it would take Jackson and whoever was with him a while to search it.

'Stay close to me,' the Doctor whispered to Amy. 'Maybe not quite that close,' he added as she stepped right up to him, shoulder to shoulder. 'There's close and there's *close*-close. Just close will do. Within reach and out of sight.'

The Doctor ducked behind the end of the line of storage banks. Carlisle was right with him, and Amy mirrored his actions a moment later. Peering out, they could just see the vague silhouettes of several figures at the other end of the cavern. The constant drip-drip of water made it difficult to hear what they were saying, but Carlisle was sure one of them was Jackson, and Reeve was with him as well. There were about half a dozen in all.

'He's brought some help,' she whispered to the Doctor.

'Pity. But never mind.' The Doctor reached his index finger and thumb into his top pocket and carefully pulled out the phial of liquid. He held it out to Amy. 'You take this,' he told her. 'If one of us can get you to the Process Chamber, it'll be better if you've got it with you. Otherwise we'll spend forever trying to get mind and body together in the same place.'

'You sure she can keep it safe?' Carlisle asked.

'Can you?' the Doctor asked Amy.

'Yes,' she said, her expression not changing.

'Good. And from now on, whisper, OK?'

'Did they hear?' Carlisle wondered. 'Someone's coming this way.'

'Not sure,' the Doctor admitted. 'Let's keep moving, try to stay ahead of them and maybe sneak past to the stairs.'

As they hurried across the next aisle and ducked into shadows, the Doctor said to Amy: 'That phial is important. Or rather, the water inside it is. I want you to keep it with you. Don't care where you keep it, so long as it stays safe and it isn't separated from you. We need to combine the data in that water with your physical embodiment at some point, OK?'

'OK,' Amy whispered back. She held the phial up to inspect it, expression still blank.

'Good. So, remember that.' The Doctor looked out, checking to see if any of Jackson's people were close by. 'Or remember as much as you can – it's a lot to swallow, I know.'

Carlisle was checking too. 'We can get to that next bay, I think.'

The Doctor nodded. 'Closer to the stairs. Come on.'

Someone was talking in the connecting aisle as they ran for the next area of cover, against the glistening, wet wall of the cavern. The searchers were closing in.

'So far, so good,' the Doctor whispered.

'Way to go yet,' Carlisle pointed out.

Beside her, the Doctor gave a sudden gasp. His mouth opened in surprise, eyes wide.

'What is it?' Carlisle asked urgently.

'Drip of water went down the back of my neck.'

'Oh, thanks for that.'

They both turned quickly as something dropped to the floor beside them. The glass phial clattered and rolled, stopping at the Doctor's feet. He scooped it up quickly.

'I told you to keep this safe,' he hissed at Amy.

'Doctor – the stopper's come off,' Carlisle said. 'It's empty.'

The Doctor held up the phial. She was right. 'Where's it gone? Where's the water?' He looked round, close to panic – there were small puddles of water all across the floor, from dripping condensation. 'Any one of these puddles could actually be Amy.'

'Shhhh!' Carlisle warned. 'Too late to worry about that now.'

'But how do we get her back?'

'Let's worry about it later, OK?' Carlisle told him. 'Right now we have to get out of here.'

'It's all clear now,' Amy whispered.

'Thank you,' the Doctor said. 'Come on then – next bay, right?'

'Right,' Carlisle agreed.

They ran as quickly and quietly as they could to the next pool of shadow. The stairway was only about fifteen metres away now. But there was a soldier standing there.

'You think he knows you've switched sides?' the Doctor asked. 'Or rather, that you haven't.'

'Probably,' Carlisle said. 'But it might be worth a try. I can distract him while you and Amy get past.'

'I don't think that will work,' Amy said.

The Doctor and Carlisle both turned towards her.

'A glimmer of self-will?' the Doctor wondered. 'Or is her programming taking hold again?'

'That's a thought,' Amy said. Suddenly, she reached out and pulled Carlisle's pistol from its holster. She aimed it at the Doctor and Carlisle.

Captain Reeve stepped out from the shadows behind Amy. He smiled with satisfaction, and called over his shoulder: 'Over here. We got them.'

'I have to trick the Doctor,' Amy said slowly. 'I have to take him to the Process Chamber.'

'Yeah, we did that bit earlier,' the Doctor told her. 'She's somehow reverted to her previous programming.' He fixed Reeve with a piercing stare. 'Maybe your process isn't all it's cracked up to be.'

'The circumstances changed and her previous programming became relevant again, that's all.'

Jackson hurried up from behind, two more soldiers with him. 'Your little excursion has saved you the ordeal of time in the hub, Doctor. Nothing more. We're ready to process you now.' He nodded to Amy. 'I'll allow Miss Pond to show you the way.'

In response, Amy jabbed the gun forwards. 'Move. Up the stairs.'

Jackson's laughter echoed round the cavern. 'We're going to the Process Chamber, Doctor. And once we get there, you will become an empty Blank, ready to be imprinted with a Talerian mind.'

Chapter
21

Hands raised, the Doctor and Carlisle walked to the dimly lit metal stairway. The soldier guarding the bottom stepped aside to allow them past. Amy was close behind them, Jackson and the others walking slowly across the cavern.

'Doctor, Major Carlisle,' Amy called to them as they started up the stairs.

They both turned to see what she wanted. The gun was steady in her hand.

'You wanted to know where the water in the phial went,' Amy said quietly. 'Well, I did what you said. I kept it close to me, I kept it safe. I drank it.'

The Doctor froze. 'You did *what*?'

'Least of our problems,' Carlisle hissed.

'But she *drank* it. I can't just stick my finger down her throat...' The Doctor hesitated, inspecting his fingers as he considered. 'No, no I can't.'

'Can't what, Doctor?' Jackson demanded as he

reached the bottom of the stairs and stood close behind Amy. 'Do enlighten us.'

As she was standing in front of him, Jackson couldn't see Amy's expressionless face relax into a smile. Then she winked.

'Whatever you do,' she said to the Doctor and Carlisle, 'don't try to... *Run!*'

On 'Run' she turned and fired the gun at the nearest light. The fluorescent tube exploded, sparks showering down.

Reeve gave a cry of surprise and anger. Jackson dashed forwards.

Amy was backing away up the stairs after the Doctor and Carlisle, aiming the gun back at the soldiers. 'You running yet?' she demanded. 'I don't hear you running.' She turned to race after them.

The Doctor and Carlisle ran, with Amy close behind. But not close enough. A hand grabbed her ankle, pulling her leg away from under her. She crashed painfully down on the metal stairs.

The Doctor turned – started back to where Reeve was dragging Amy down the steps.

But Carlisle grabbed his arm. 'We can't help her if we're all caught. With us free she has a chance – come on!'

They took the rest of the stairs two at a time, hearing the booted feet of the soldiers echoing after them. The door at the top had been smashed open. The Doctor pulled it shut again behind them, heaving and jamming it in place.

'They got Amy,' he said. But he was grinning like a maniac. 'She's OK – she got her mind back.'

'Seems so. Because she drank the water?'

'Must be,' the Doctor said. He scratched his head, exciting his hair into spikes. 'They must be using a holographic storage model. The complete dataset is repeated in every tiny drop of water. Like if you break a hologram, each broken piece doesn't just show a broken part of the whole like a jigsaw puzzle. They each hold a smaller version of the complete picture. How diluted must that data have been by the time it hit her bloodstream? But her brain managed to get the information out and rebuild her mind. Filled in the blanks.' He shook his head in awe. 'You humans are wonderful.'

The door trembled and shook as someone tried to wrench it open from the other side.

'Doctor,' Carlisle said with exaggerated patience, 'I'm very happy for Amy, and I'm glad you know all about holograms. But she's a prisoner – they'll just blank her again and this time they might not keep a copy. Plus we're trapped on a base on the dark side of the moon that's been taken over by invading aliens. Maybe we should get away from here before they open that door?'

There was a wrenching, scraping sound from the door. It opened a centimetre, then jammed again.

'I suppose,' the Doctor agreed. 'But we're not going far. As soon as they're out, I need to go back down there.'

'But we just escaped from back down there.'

The Doctor strode off down the corridor. 'Yes, but that was before I had a plan.'

Carlisle hurried after him. 'And now you do?'

The Doctor spun round and grabbed Carlisle's shoulders, looking her right in the face. 'Oh *boy*, do I have a plan,' he said.

They waited in a storeroom off the main corridor. Carlisle assured the Doctor that Jackson and the others would have to pass this way en route from the cavern housing the computer facility to the Process Chamber.

The Doctor held the door open just a fraction. He sat cross-legged on the floor, looking out. Carlisle stood beside him, also watching.

They didn't have to wait very long before Jackson strode angrily past, followed by Reeve. Several soldiers escorted Amy after them. She looked glum but defiant.

'See you soon, Pond,' the Doctor murmured.

'I was afraid you were about to mount a daring but foolhardy rescue attempt,' Carlisle said after they'd gone.

The Doctor eased the door open. 'I am. But not in the way they expect.'

'So what do we do?'

The Doctor checked both ways along the corridor before stepping out of the room. 'I assume you know where the controls are for the fire-fighting systems.'

Carlisle nodded. 'Main control room. Why?'

'Because that's where I need you to be.'

'You want me to make sure the fire control systems don't work?'

'No no no. That's the last thing I want.' The Doctor took a deep breath, sucking air through his teeth. 'I want you to make sure no one can override the system and turn it off.'

'And where will you be? Starting a fire?'

'Only a metaphorical one.'

Carlisle frowned. 'Do you ever explain anything properly?'

'All right, you want an explanation? I'll keep it simple. If you take a glass of water, right? And you throw it into the ocean, OK?'

'The glass?'

'Just the water in the glass. Well, doesn't matter for the explanation, but throwing stuff other than water into the sea isn't generally good. Now you mix up the ocean, let's just pretend you can do that, so that the glass of water you just threw in is mixed in with all the other water – millions of billions of litres of water.'

'With the water from my glass in there somewhere all mixed up. So what?'

'So now comes the clever part. You take the glass you didn't throw in as well, and you scoop out another glassful of water from the same ocean. Doesn't matter where from. What have you got?'

Carlisle blinked, then shrugged. 'A glass of salty water, I guess.'

'Exactly. But in that water, mixed in somewhere, is just a tiny part – a few molecules – of the *same glass of water* you started with. Guaranteed.'

Major Carlisle thought about that. 'You sure?'

'Of course I'm sure.'

'Have you, like, done it?'

The Doctor's eyes narrowed. 'Yes.'

'Liar.'

'OK, so no, I haven't actually done it as such. But there are so many molecules of water in that one glass that you'd get some of them back again no matter where you scooped out your second glass.'

'And this somehow relates to your plan?'

'It does.'

Carlisle nodded. 'Well, I hope you know what you're doing, because I still don't have a clue.'

'I know what I'm doing,' the Doctor told her confidently. 'I'm just not sure if it will work.'

There was no point in fighting. Amy had tried that last time and it did no good. She needed to slow them down to give the Doctor as much time as possible to rescue her. She knew he would, somehow. She walked as slowly as she dared. She took her time getting into the chair on the Process Chamber. She clenched her muscles, hoping that would leave some slack after they tied the straps.

Nurse Phillips watched her. Judging by her smile, she was obviously enjoying Amy's predicament.

'There will be some pain,' she said. 'I'm sure you'll remember.'

'I'll remember all right,' Amy told her. 'And you've been through it too, you know.'

'Not me. This body, but not *me*.'

'That's enough,' Jackson snapped. 'Start setting things up. Full transmission will start soon, and I want her blanked before that and ready to receive the next available Talerian.'

Jackson took over from the nurse, strapping Amy's

ankles first. Amy just smiled.

'He'll stop you,' she said quietly, surprised at how confident she sounded. 'He always does.'

Jackson didn't answer. But he hesitated just long enough for Amy to know he was worried. He flinched as the phone on the wall buzzed.

'Probably him now,' Amy said. 'Don't keep him waiting.'

'Quiet!' Jackson snarled. He crossed the room and picked up the phone. 'Yes?'

Amy watched Jackson frown.

'He's what? But that makes no sense at all, what's he doing down there?' Jackson listened for a while before answering. 'I have no idea, but you'd better get down there and stop him. We don't need his body, we'll soon have plenty of those. It's a pity, because the Doctor's body would make a good receptacle. But he has become more trouble than his body is worth. So kill him.' Jackson slammed the phone back on to its cradle.

Amy was at once full of excitement and trepidation. Did the Doctor know they'd discovered whatever he was up to? Knowing him, that could be part of his plan. But then again, knowing the Doctor, it might not have occurred to him at all...

'It's started,' she said calmly. 'I told you, you've got no chance.'

Jackson yanked the straps tight around her wrists.

There were too many of them in the Control Room. Carlisle knew from the computer index that almost all of the soldiers had been taken over. To make matters worse, Captain Reeve was there. She'd hoped he'd gone to the Process Chamber with Jackson, but here he was using the security cameras to try to find the Doctor.

It wasn't long before one of the soldiers spotted the Doctor heading back towards the Computer Facility. Reeve called Jackson, and then hurried out, taking all but one of the soldiers with him.

Carlisle didn't have time to worry about the Doctor. She had a job to do, and for the first time since she'd woken up strapped into the chair in the Process Chamber, she felt in control.

The soldier turned as she entered the Control Room. Major Carlisle smiled at him, and he nodded and turned back to his work.

A moment later, he seemed to realise who had just come in. 'Hang on –'

The soldier started to turn in his seat, reaching for his sidearm. But Major Carlisle's own gun thumped into the side of his head, sending him sprawling across the control console.

'Getting to be a habit,' she murmured as she shifted the soldier's unconscious body out of the way and set about accessing the fire suppression systems.

'Step away from the controls, Doctor.' Reeve's shout echoed round the cavern. 'Now! Or I'll shoot you dead where you stand.'

The Doctor punched a final key, nodded with satisfaction, and stepped aside. Reeve and several soldiers came running up.

'What have you done?' Reeve demanded.

'Not much. Just changed some routings.'

One of the soldiers was typing rapidly, watching the display screen as he displayed a log of recent actions.

'Well?' Reeve demanded.

'He's changed the flow, opened some valves, accessed computer storage.' The soldier shook his head. 'Doesn't make any sense. It looks from this like he's vented the inert gas from the fire systems and filled the tank with…' The soldier checked the readings in a smaller window on the screen. 'With water from the reservoir, and also from data storage.'

'What data did he use?' Reeve held his gun close to the Doctor's face. 'I hope you think it was worth it.'

'I think it was worth it,' the Doctor said.

The soldier looked up at Reeve. 'He used the back-ups. The water storing all the human mind imprints.'

'The Doctor was looking distinctly pleased with himself. 'That's right. You're all in there, I'm pleased to say. All mixed up together in the fire suppression tank. Molecules swirling round. The tiniest part of your data in every drip and drop of water in there.'

Reeve laughed. 'I don't know what you thought you were doing, but you've destroyed them. You've killed all those people you were so desperate to save.'

'You think so?' the Doctor murmured.

Reeve glanced away, just for a second, sharing the joke with the other soldiers. Just a second, but it was all the Doctor needed. He whipped out his sonic screwdriver and pointed it at the nearest fire alarm – on the opposite wall.

The small glass panel on the alarm point shattered. A siren cut in immediately. The display screen the soldier was using flashed up a message:

```
Fire Alert - Inert Gas Sprinklers
            Activated.
```

'It'll take a little while for the water to get along the pipes to the sprinklers,' the Doctor said. He almost had to shout to be heard above the alarm. 'Major Carlisle should have locked open all the internal doors and bulkheads, and rigged it so all the sprinklers will go off, not just the ones in this area. I also opened a constant flow from the main reservoir so there'll be plenty of water.'

'You're mad,' Reeve said. 'If Jackson had wiped your mind, he'd have done you a favour. As it is, he won't need to.'

Reeve took a step back. He gripped his gun in both hands, aiming straight at the Doctor. On the far side of the cavern, water burst from a roof-mounted sprinkler. Then from another, and another. All across the vast space, water fell like rain.

'I might have known you didn't really have a plan at all,' Reeve said. His finger tightened on the trigger.

'I have a brilliant plan. The only downside...' the Doctor told Reeve as a sprinkler directly above showered water down around them '... is that we all get wet.'

'The only downside,' Reeve retorted, 'is that you die.' He pulled the trigger. The sound of the gunshot echoed off the rock walls.

Chapter
22

The water was cold on her face, running down her cheeks like tears. Major Carlisle stared at the monitor showing the images from several security cameras in astonishment.

'How in hell has he done that?' she said out loud. She laughed. 'That's brilliant. Bizarre, but brilliant.' She had to get back to the computer facility and ask him to explain what was going on. No, she decided, first she had to get to the Process Chamber and check that Amy was all right.

Carlisle ran from the control room. The images from the cameras showed soldiers and scientists all round the base – just standing absolutely still. Their heads were nodded forwards, as if they had simply fallen asleep.

'I am so glad to see you,' Amy said as Major Carlisle undid the straps holding her into the chair. 'How did the Doctor do it? No, forget that – first tell me *what* he's done.'

The last strap came free, and Carlisle stepped back to let Amy out of the process chair. Nearby, a soldier stood lazily as if he was asleep. His head was nodded forward on his chest and his eyes were closed. Water from the sprinklers ran down his face and dripped from his hair.

'Don't ask me,' Carlisle said. 'Everyone's like this. Nurse Phillips is the same in the observation room, just like the guards outside.'

'Everyone except Jackson,' Amy told her. 'He legged it when the guard there got the slumps. It's like…' She rubbed furiously at her wrists to try to get some circulation back. 'It's like that soldier was when he blanked out after sabotaging the systems.'

'Is that what the Doctor's done? Blanked them all again somehow?'

'Let's ask him. And he needs to know it didn't work on Jackson, so come on.'

'Let's hope we can turn these sprinklers off soon.'

They passed several soldiers on the way. All of them were slumped forward, as if sleeping. By the time they reached the cavern, Amy and Carlisle were both completely drenched.

'I'll never be dry again,' Amy complained.

'I suppose it *is* just water,' Carlisle said as they started down the steps. Water ran and dripped through the metal mesh of the treads under their feet.

'Oh thanks for that,' Amy said. 'Goodness knows how much of it I've swallowed.'

'But it hasn't affected us.'

'Apart from making us wet. Still…' Amy said as they reached the bottom of the step and saw the Doctor. Despite the situation, she couldn't stop herself from laughing at the sight. 'Could be worse.'

He was holding up Captain Reeve's slumped body from behind, standing directly under a sprinkler head. The water splashed and cascaded off the two of them. The Doctor's hair was plastered down the side of his face, covering one eye. He glared at Amy.

'It's not *that* funny,' he said.

'What are you doing?' Amy shouted above the sound of the water.

'If I let him go, he'll fall.'

'You shouldn't have moved him,' Carlisle said. 'The others are balanced all right.'

Several soldiers were standing close by, heads bowed and shoulders slumped. Another was sprawled forwards over a keyboard and display screen.

'I was just doing a little experiment,' the Doctor said. 'Here help me put him down. Yes, here, under the sprinkler. I want him to get a really good dose. Let's see if it speeds things up.'

Carlisle carefully removed the pistol from Reeve's hand.

'Bit late for that,' the Doctor told her. 'He's already taken his shot.'

'What? Where?' Amy exclaimed. 'Are you hurt?'

'No, he missed. It was just as the effect of the water got to him. Lucky for me. He slumped forward and the shot bounced off the floor somewhere.'

'So don't keep us in suspense,' Amy said. 'What is

it with this water? Why are they all blanked out?'

'Their minds are trying desperately to adapt.'

On the floor between them, Reeve groaned and moved, curling into a protective ball.

'Looks like it's working,' the Doctor went on.

'What did you do?' Carlisle asked. 'What's in the water?'

'*They* are. Their minds, at least. Remember what I said about a glass of water in the ocean? I mixed all the water containing the backed-up minds into the tank that's feeding the sprinklers. Just like Amy's own brain managed to latch on to her mind imprint when she drank her back-up, Captain Reeve is absorbing the tiniest part of his own mind through his skin.'

'In the water from the sprinklers,' Carlisle realised. 'Holograms.'

'You what?' Amy said. 'Look, am I the only person here who speaks human?'

'The whole of the mind-print encoded in every molecule,' the Doctor explained. 'Every drop of water that touches us contains the diluted mind-prints of everyone Jackson wiped. The first effect is to purge the brain of the alien influence, it's rejected as the human brain struggles to reabsorb its own pattern from the water.'

Reeve was uncurling now and trying to sit up. He looked round in confusion.

'The more water that hits the skin, the quicker the process,' the Doctor said triumphantly.

'Um, one obvious question,' Amy said. 'If everyone's mind is in every drop of water, how does Reeve's brain know which data to absorb? Won't he get a bit of everyone's mind? Won't that make him one crazy, mixed-up person?'

The Doctor smiled and clasped his hands together behind his back. 'No, that's the clever thing. Because the brain should be able to identify its own mind-print and just take the data that belongs to it. Like recognising your own car in amongst hundreds in the supermarket car park.'

'I often get the wrong car,' Carlisle told him.

Amy walked slowly round the Doctor. He turned to keep facing towards her. 'You've got your fingers crossed behind your back, haven't you?' she said accusingly.

The Doctor's smile became slightly fixed. 'Might have.'

'You have no idea if this is going to work or not?'

'The theory's sound,' he protested. 'Mostly.'

Carlisle gestured to Captain Reeve, now getting groggily to his feet. 'I think we're about to find out.'

Reeve was looking round, confused.

'He'll be fine,' the Doctor said. 'Really – fine.'

'Who in blazes are you?' Reeve demanded. 'What am I doing down here?'

'He's confused,' Amy said. 'Maybe it hasn't worked.'

'No, it's just that the real Captain Reeve never met us,' the Doctor told her. 'We didn't arrive until after he'd been blanked.'

'Major?' Reeve asked. 'What's going on?'

'It's a bit tricky to explain,' Carlisle admitted. 'But it's good to have you back, Captain Reeve.'

'What's the last thing you remember?' the Doctor

asked, shining his sonic screwdriver in Reeve's startled face.

'I was with Professor Jackson and Nurse Phillips, in the Process Chamber. They wanted me to look at something. Then…' He shook his head. 'Then this. What's happening?'

'Alien invasion,' the Doctor said. 'Don't worry about it. But we'll need your help.'

Reeve looked at the three of them: the Doctor grinning manically; Amy smiling in relief and amusement; the usually ice-calm Carlisle as drenched as the rest of them as the water continued to shower down. 'And you wondered if I was mad,' he said.

Amy was starting to shiver. She was soaked through. 'Can't we turn the sprinklers off now?'

'Seems so,' the Doctor said. 'Now that everyone's blanked out.' He turned and headed for the stairs, splashing through the deepening puddles.

'Except Jackson,' Carlisle pointed out.

The Doctor froze in mid step. 'What?'

'It didn't seem to affect Jackson,' Amy confirmed. 'He did a runner. Probably hiding out somewhere, or having a calming cup of that tea of his while he plots his next fiendish move. I mean, there's not much he can do on his own, is there?'

'Why didn't it affect Jackson?' the Doctor demanded. He stared accusingly at Reeve.

'Don't ask me,' he protested. 'You're the expert. I just got here, remember.'

The Doctor was running again, but this time towards the aisles of data storage. His foot slapped down in a puddle close to Amy, splashing her legs.

'Oh cheers.'

The Doctor ignored her, frantically pulling open drawers in the huge cabinets. The others hurried to join him. Amy was in time to see him pause as he opened one drawer. They were full of phials of colourless liquid.

'The phials are all connected to the main systems. I pumped all the water out and into the tank for the sprinklers. Then they get refilled from main storage... If Jackson's phial was in here, he must have been mixed in with the others.'

The Doctor barely glanced at the contents of the drawer before slamming it shut again. He pulled open the next drawer down, and they all saw that one of the phials was missing.

'It's OK, that's you, Amy.' The Doctor turned and grinned at her. 'I did a pond water joke. Probably not worth repeating though.' He pushed the drawer shut again. The next drawer down was full, and the next.

Before long, the Doctor had moved to the next cabinet. Three drawers down, another phial was missing. The Doctor tapped the empty slot with his finger. 'Want to bet that's the real Professor Jackson?'

The Control Room was the best place to start looking for Jackson, Major Carlisle suggested. They could also turn off the sprinklers before the base flooded. The Doctor sent Captain Reeve to check on the prisoners in the hub.

'They were all blanked by Jackson in the last few days. I'm hoping the sprinkler systems work over in the cells too and it isn't a separate system.'

'Should do,' Reeve said. 'But I'll go take a look.'

Only certain parts of the base were covered by security cameras. Once she'd turned off the sprinklers, Carlisle checked each camera's image in turn. Most showed soldiers and staff standing slumped from the effects of the water. There was no sign of Jackson.

'How long before they start to recover properly?' Amy wondered, looking at the soldier collapsed across the end of the main control console.

'Shouldn't be too long. The ones closest to sprinklers should start to wake up first, like Reeve. Though he drank quite a lot too, I think. His mouth was open because he was threatening me when he blanked out.'

'I thought he was shooting you,' Carlisle said.

'That too. He was multi-tasking.'

Their conversation was interrupted by an insistent bleeping from one of the consoles.

'Local radio signal,' Carlisle said. 'Who can that be?' She worked the controls and a voice echoed out of nearby speakers:

'...repeat, this is Lieutenant Ashton passing over Base Diana. Can anyone hear me? Come in, please, Base Diana.'

The Doctor took the microphone. 'Oh, hi, this is the Doctor. Good to know you're OK. We seem to have things pretty much under control down here. How are you?'

'I'm fine,' Ashton replied. 'Good to know you're all sorted. Just one thing...'

'You want to know when you can head home?' the Doctor suggested.

'Apart from that. There's like, lightning up here. I don't know how else to describe it.'

'Lightning?' Amy said. 'Is that possible? I mean, in space?'

The Doctor rubbed his wet hair vigorously. 'Not really. Not *lightning* lightning. What's it look like?'

'A streak of light,' Ashton said. 'Like someone's turned on a huge searchlight. I can see it shining across space. Brilliant white light, I can barely look it's so bright.'

'And where's it shining?' Carlisle asked.

'That's just it. It's shining right at Base Diana. Right at *you*.'

There was silence for several moments. The Doctor's frown deepened.

Finally, Ashton spoke again: 'Hey, look, I'm going to be passing round the other side of the moon in a couple of minutes, so we'll lose contact. But I thought you should know. I'll leave that with you guys, OK?'

Carlisle told him to call in again on his next orbit, and cut the connection.

'What is it?' Amy asked the Doctor. 'Something Jackson's done?'

'Their Plan B,' the Doctor said gravely. 'Should have guessed they'd have one. Jackson's sent them a message and told them to forget thought pattern transference now that we've un-blanked their people here.'

'But, that's good isn't it?' Carlisle said.

'Not good,' the Doctor replied. 'Not if I'm right about that light beam.'

'Why, what is it?'

'I think it's a concentrated stream of data. They're not just transferring consciousness and brain wave patterns this time.'

The main screen was still displaying the view from one of the security cameras. It showed an intersection of several corridors. Two soldiers were slumped by a doorway.

In the middle of the intersection, the air seemed to shimmer. A vague shape was forming within the trembling air. Shadows darkened and became more substantial. The shimmer faded, and in its place stood a figure.

The creature was about the same height as a man. But the limbs were swollen and smooth. Its head was joined directly to the body with no neck, poking out of the plates of metallic body armour that hung round the creature's torso. A single, huge oval-shaped eye stared out from a bulbous head that was breaking out into glutinous pustules. Stubby clawed fingers clutched a brutal-looking gun made of grey metal.

Slime dripped from the creature's pale green skin as it walked slowly towards the camera. It paused for a moment, as if staring into the Control Room. A hole opened beneath its eye – a wide slash of a mouth, filled with ragged teeth. It raised its glutinous, clawed hands, aiming the gun at the camera. The end of the weapon glowed a livid red, and the screen blacked out.

'I thought it was just increased bandwidth to send through more Talerian minds. But actually it's a matter transmission beam. Looks like the Talerians are here in force,' the Doctor said quietly. 'And in person.'

The door to the Control Room slammed open. In the doorway stood another of the bulbous, slimy creatures. Its mouth split into what might have been a smile, and it raised its gun.

Chapter

23

As soon as the hideous creature appeared in the doorway, Major Carlisle hurled herself across the room. Her shoulder knocked the gun sideways. A blast of energy hurtled across the room and exploded on the wall, sending out sparks.

The Talerian's slimy hide was contracted as Carlisle cannoned into the creature's armour, pressing it into the skin. But the skin was tightly sprung, like the surface of a balloon, and she found herself bouncing off, and crashing to the floor.

With a roar of anger, the creature took several squelching steps forwards. It raised its gun again. Amy dragged Carlisle back, while the Doctor watched with apparent interest.

'You'll probably want to keep us alive,' he told the Talerian. 'Jackson, or whatever his real name is, wants to wipe our minds.'

The creature hesitated, gun still aimed at Carlisle

as Amy helped her up. Then it gave another roar, and fired.

At the same moment, the blanked and unconscious soldier sprawled across the control console groaned and straightened up. Distracted, the creature turned towards the movement. Again, its shot went wide – blasting part of the console to pieces. The soldier stared in shocked amazement.

Amy hurled the nearest thing she could find at the creature – a coffee cup. Cold dregs of coffee dripped from the cup as it turned in the air. But, like Carlisle, it just bounced off the creature's armour.

The recovering soldier's training cut in, overcoming his shock in a moment. He picked up the chair from beside the console, raised it, and charged. The wheeled base of the chair hammered into the Talerian, forcing it backwards. It bumped heavily into the wall, its whole body shimmering like jelly and armour plates rattling.

His momentum kept the soldier going. Amy stared in fascinated horror as the chair's base squashed into the creature's belly. One of the wheels on the chair was jammed between two of the loose armour plates, stretching the skin behind inwards like it was made of thin rubber. Any moment, the skin would spring back into shape and the soldier would he hurled off like he'd fallen on to a trampoline.

Except it didn't happen. The sharp surround of the wheel cut into the Talerian's skin. It pierced the rubbery hide – making the smallest of holes. But it was enough.

With a rumbling, gurgling, anguished cry, the

Talerian *burst*. Grey-green gunge erupted from its punctured skin and the whole body seemed to deflate. The bulbous arms flailed aimlessly, before losing their form and substance. The gun clattered to the floor. In a few seconds, all that was left was a pool of gooey liquid and metallic, armoured plates lying across the shrivelled-up hide of the creature, like a deflated balloon.

'Well that answers one of my questions,' the Doctor said. He knelt down beside the creature's remains. He dipped his finger in the goo, and for one awful moment Amy was afraid he was going to lick it. But instead he sniffed at it curiously, then wiped it off again on the lapel of his jacket.

'What question is that?' Carlisle wondered. She looked pale and shaken – but nowhere near as confused and shocked as the soldier, still holding the gunge-spattered chair.

'Why they want human bodies. Their own are obviously far too fragile. Humans, for all your failings, really are quite robust. Not like viscous liquid-based creatures such as Mr Blobby-Balloon here.'

'How many of them are there?' Amy asked. 'And what do we do – throw darts at them?'

'You got any darts?' the Doctor said.

'Well, no.'

'Not really an option then, is it?'

They all looked up as a bing-bong chime sounded.

'Public address system,' Carlisle explained. 'Never known it used before, though.'

Jackson's voice came through loud and clear. 'This

is Androparg to all Talerian forces. Commander Raraarg has decreed that we need the humans alive as mind-fodder for our initial strike force to infiltrate planet Earth. Make sure all weapons are set to stun. And be careful, some of the Blanks are waking up and going rogue.' There was a pause before Jackson added: 'And to any humans listening – surrender or you will be shot. That is all.'

The voice cut out.

'Charming,' Amy decided.

'We know where he is now,' Carlisle said, checking the control console. 'That was broadcast from Jackson's office.'

The Doctor clapped his hands together. 'Terrific. Then it's obvious what we do. You and you...' He pointed to Carlisle and then to the still bemused soldier. '... Find Captain Reeve and get everyone together somewhere you can defend. The canteen would be good, because then you can get croissants and hot drinks and those buns with the slightly cinnamon flavour.'

'What about you and me?' Amy asked.

'We're continuing with the hot drink theme – by going for a cup of tea with Professor Jackson and Commander Raraarg.'

All across the base, soldiers and other staff were waking up, confused and disorientated. Jackson's announcement did nothing to help them adjust. Captain Reeve found several soldiers close to the hub where the prisoners were kept and together they opened the cells and ordered the prisoners out.

As soon as the first emaciated man stepped out of his cell, Reeve could tell they'd been neglected since Jackson took charge of the prison facility. The Captain was appalled at the way they had been treated since he'd been blanked – they'd obviously been given precious little food or water and probably denied their usual exercise time.

'Get these people to the canteen,' he ordered. 'They need a decent meal before anything else.' He turned to the nearest prisoner, shuffling towards him. 'What's your name?'

'I'll tell you nothing,' the man rasped, his voice a dry whisper. 'You have no right to keep me here.'

Reeve nodded. That told him all he needed to know – the man's mind was his own. 'Well, whoever you are, let the other prisoners know that we're taking you to the canteen for something to eat. I'm sorry you've been treated badly, but we have a situation here. I can't tell you any more than that.'

The man stared back at him, wide-eyed. 'Would this situation involve *that*?' He pointed past Reeve.

Reeve turned – to see the bulbous, slimy shape of a Talerian sludging towards them. Reeve instinctively reached for his gun. But his holster was empty – the gun lying on the floor in the cavernous computer facility.

'Halt!' he shouted. 'Halt – or my men will fire.'

It was an empty threat. The soldiers on the base were not routinely armed, and none of them had weapons. The Talerian was brandishing its own gun. The end glowed and a beam of energy shot out – slamming one of the soldiers back against the glass window running the length of the room. He slumped unconscious to the floor.

Soldiers and prisoners dived for cover as the alien creature advanced. Then, suddenly, the Talerian exploded in a squelch of viscous grey-green liquid.

Behind the steaming remains, Major Carlisle stood holding one of the alien weapons.

'Are you sure this is the way?' Amy asked as they started down yet another corridor. They all looked the same to her. All the doors were open, she noticed – part of the Doctor's plan with the fire systems so the sprinklers would go off throughout the base.

'Depends where you think we're going.'

'Jackson's office?'

The Doctor made a noncommittal sound.

'You're lost, aren't you?'

He made the same sound again. Ahead of them, the bulbous figure of a Talerian stepped out of an open doorway. It didn't see them as it walked with a blubbery gait away down the corridor.

'There we are – just what we need,' the Doctor said happily. 'Come on.' He hurried to catch up with the alien.

'What?' Amy mouthed. 'What are you doing?' she hissed as she caught him up.

'Asking directions.' The Doctor quickened his pace. 'I know, men generally don't, but Time Lords aren't proud. At least, not this one. Oi – you there!' he called. 'Yes, you with the blobby face and one eye.'

The Talerian stopped and slowly turned towards them, raising its gun. It gave a gargling noise that might have been surprise or laughter.

'Glad we found you,' the Doctor said. 'Jackson wants to see us. You'll know him as Androparg. So if you could just point us in the right direction?'

The Talerian jabbed its gun towards them.

'Or show us,' Amy said quickly. 'That'd be great. Oh, you coming too?'

'There'll be tea,' the Doctor promised. 'Maybe biscuits. I probably have a jammy dodger of my own somewhere. Usually do.' He patted his pockets. 'No?'

They passed several more Talerians on the way. But quite the largest and most revolting Talerian that Amy had so far seen was waiting inside Jackson's office. Professor Jackson himself was sitting at his desk. Even with the grotesque, glutinous alien standing close by watching them, Amy was again impressed by the view out of the large window behind Jackson. Bathed in pale evening sunlight, the grey moon looked somehow warm and majestic rather than colourless and desolate.

'You must be Raraarg,' the Doctor said with delight. He held out his hand, regarded the alien's blobby appendage, and decided: 'Maybe not.'

'What an unexpected pleasure,' Jackson said. He dismissed the Talerian who had brought them and looked from the Doctor to Amy and back again. 'You've come to surrender?'

'We came for tea, actually,' the Doctor told him. 'I assume the offer still stands?'

The huge Talerian leader shuddered and growled.

'Tea,' Jackson mused. 'I had to drink it at first to maintain the illusion that I was still Jackson. But now I actually find it quite pleasant. I must confess it's one of the few things I find invigorates this rather strange body I have acquired.'

'That'll be the caffeine and tannin,' the Doctor said. 'I'm sure it's good for the soul.' He turned to the Talerian leader Raraarg. 'You should try it.'

This provoked more growls and wobbles.

'No,' the Doctor agreed. 'It might upset your rather delicate insides, mightn't it? Must be a problem having a balloon body like that. Any little wound and you don't bleed, you *rupture*. Any change in atmospheric pressure and you either squash up and implode, or the internal pressure makes you explode. I can see why you might envy humans. But you can't just take their bodies, you know.'

'Why not?' Jackson asked.

'Because you can't,' Amy told him. 'It's not right. It's not fair. Its murder, that's why.'

'What does Professor Jackson think about it?' the Doctor asked. 'I assume he's still inside you somewhere. As the first to be taken over, you'd need to preserve his memories and emotions so you could survive undetected. If you'd just blanked out, people would notice. Worse than just forgetting names – you'd have forgotten everything.'

Jackson nodded. 'He's in here.' He tapped his forehead. 'Just. The tiniest hint of him. And he knows it. I can feel what's left of his mind struggling to reassert itself. But you know what? It gets fainter and more desperate all the time. And soon, he'll be gone completely.'

'Except for his back-up. I assume there is a back-up?'

Jackson smiled. 'You know there is.' He pulled open a drawer in the desk and took out a glass phial of colourless liquid. 'I could have destroyed it. But that really would be murder.' He set the phial down on the desk in front of him. 'The human mind...' he mused.

'Plus you never knew if you might need him back, did you. You still might – if his equipment goes wrong, or some memory you need has faded away.'

'There is that.'

'So what happens now?' Amy asked, glancing apprehensively at the shuddering alien beside them. 'Your blob-men won't win against trained soldiers.'

'You'd be surprised,' Jackson said. 'We can wait, and more Talerian troops are on the way. This is just the first wave. As soon as I boost the signal from Jackson's process equipment, the main force will latch on to it and transfer here from Taleria.'

'Just as you latched on to it in the first place, I assume?' the Doctor prompted.

Jackson smiled thinly. 'Jackson – the real Jackson – didn't even realise his process was emitting a signal. It was faint, but it was enough. Our bodies are dying, Doctor. Every generation of Talerians is born more fragile than the one before. We are constantly looking for a new form, a replacement for our frail structure. Imagine my sense of euphoria when my mind was transported along the link and I woke to find myself inside this.' He spread his arms.

'You too can have a body like mine,' Amy quipped.

'I won't pretend it was easy,' Jackson said. 'It took me a while to get control of Jackson's consciousness and take over completely. There were mistakes and problems.'

'Like poor Liz Didbrook,' the Doctor said.

'The process never completed,' Jackson told them. 'But that has been corrected. I boosted the signal, and ensured the next transfers would be perfect.'

'So if we turn off all Jackson's equipment,' Amy said, 'we can stop any more of you turning up out of the blue.'

The Talerian beside her roared with what sounded unsettlingly like laughter.

'We control the Process Chamber. Major Carlisle and Captain Reeve would never get there alive.'

In a sudden fury, the Doctor shoved aside the chair in front of Jackson's desk. He leaned right over the desk and stared into Jackson's face. 'What gives you the right to take another life form's body? What do you really think you can achieve?'

Jackson stared back at the Doctor, unflinching. 'When you've quite finished.'

'Oh I haven't started yet.' The Doctor slowly straightened up, one half of his jacket trailing back across the desk. 'I came for tea, remember?'

'Enjoy your tea, Doctor,' Jackson said. 'And you, Miss Pond. Very soon we'll round up the humans and simply start to process them all again. All except you, Doctor. Yes, you can have your tea. Let's call it a last request, shall we?'

'Oh, let's not,' the Doctor said quietly.

'But it is, I'm afraid. You see, as soon as you've finished, you will die.' From behind the desk, Jackson lifted one of the Talerian weapons and aimed it right at the Doctor. 'You'll die knowing you've failed, and that Miss Pond is next in the queue for the process. On its maximum setting, this gun can blast through armour plate. Let's see what it does to a body, shall we?'

Chapter
24

The canteen had been turned into a fortress. All but one of the doors were barricaded shut, tables and chairs piled against them. When Major Carlisle overrode the fire systems, she'd locked all the doors open so they'd had to physically force them closed.

Soldiers, scientists and prisoners sat on the floor or stood in small groups. Nurse Phillips was at a table, tending to several minor injuries. The only open door was guarded by Major Carlisle and several other soldiers.

'They must have worked out where we are and what we're doing by now,' Liz Didbrook said. She was looking pale and tired. But her head was clear at last of the alien presence that had tried to force its way inside her mind.

Carlisle had to agree. 'When Captain Reeve gets back, we block this door.'

'Then what?'

'Then we wait for the Doctor and Amy.'

At some point, Carlisle realised, she'd moved from hope to belief. There was no doubt in her mind that the Doctor would sort things out. It was strange how she trusted the man, almost despite his appearance and youth. There was a wealth of experience behind his eyes and she dared not think how he had come by it. What he had faced. What he had done...

The sound of running feet signalled the return of Reeve and his team. They had gone in search of as many people as they could find – directing them to get to the canteen as quickly and cautiously as possible.

'There are blob-men right behind us,' Reeve warned. 'Not too many, luckily as most of them seem to be guarding the Process Chamber.'

'Maybe that's where they'll bring in their reinforcements,' Carlisle guessed.

'We could take the fight to them,' Reeve suggested. 'We have two of their guns now.'

She shook her head. 'We stay put, like the Doctor said. But we'll keep this door clear in case we get a chance to do something. Or we need to evacuate.'

'At least we know bullets stop them,' Captain Reeve said. He checked his handgun. 'Not that we have many left. And they've sealed off the armoury. We won't get any more ammunition.'

The first of the Talerians oozed into view along the corridor. Several others followed cautiously, guns at the ready, plates of armour rattling as they moved. An energy blast seared past Reeve and blew a chunk out of the door frame.

'Then we need to make every bullet count,' Carlisle said.

The Doctor busied himself at the tea urn as if he and Amy really had just popped into Jackson's office for a chat and refreshments. He lifted the lid and sniffed at the Earl Grey. He took a long-handled spoon from a small rack nearby and stirred the brew slowly and thoroughly.

'Sure you won't?' he asked Amy.

'Not without milk, thanks.'

The Doctor turned to the Talerian leader, Raraarg. 'And I assume you'll give it a miss. If you ever took on human form, you'd want to try it though.' The Doctor held a cup under the urn and turned the tap. 'Not that you'll get the chance.'

Having poured a second cup, the Doctor walked back to the desk. He passed a cup of tea to Jackson, then pulled up the chair he'd moved aside earlier and plonked himself down on it with a relaxed 'Aaah!'

Raraarg was wobbling ominously and emitting irritated squelching growls.

Jackson smiled indulgently and sipped his own tea. 'Don't worry,' he told his leader. 'This will be over soon.'

'Not too hot, I hope?' the Doctor asked politely.

'Just how I like it, thank you.'

The Doctor set his tea down on the desk and leaned back in the chair. 'So, last chance time, then.' He tilted his head so he could look at both Raraarg and Jackson. 'Are you going to surrender and retreat, never to darken these skies again?'

Jackson laughed. 'Very droll, Doctor. But I'm afraid it's over.'

'You are so right,' the Doctor said.

'That's a "No" then, is it?' Amy asked. She had no idea what the Doctor was doing, but he was up to something.

Raraarg let out a menacing, throaty growl. The creature's eye rolled angrily. The meaning was obvious – 'Kill him now!'

Jackson held up his hand. 'In a moment, I promise you.'

'He doesn't know, does he?' the Doctor said.

Jackson frowned. 'Doesn't know what?'

'Last chance – surrender or suffer the consequences.'

Raraarg squelched towards the Doctor.

Jackson drained his tea and set the cup down on the desk next to the glass phial still standing there. He raised the gun again. 'There will definitely be consequences,' he said.

'What doesn't our globby friend know?' Amy prompted.

The Doctor was smiling. 'He doesn't know he's been tricked. He doesn't know that Professor Jackson isn't a Talerian at all. It's not us who are being held prisoner here...' He turned towards the shimmering blob. 'It's *you.*'

The Talerian swung round to stare accusingly at Jackson.

'He's bluffing,' Jackson said. 'I boosted the signal and opened the pathway so you could bring in the attack force. This is his last pathetic attempt to...'

Jackson blinked rapidly several times, hesitating as if trying to find the right words. '... to confuse us. To turn us against one another.' He leaned forward glaring at the Doctor across the desk through his pale blue eyes.

'Yes?' the Doctor prompted. 'Something to tell me?'

'Only that your time is up. I told you that Jackson's mind is completely suppressed by my own.'

'So you did. I remember that.'

'And I have the back-up copy safely here.' He pointed at the small glass phial standing next to the cup on the desk.

'So you do. I can see that.'

'You mean that phial?' Amy said. She frowned. There was something about it, now she came to look. 'That *empty* phial,' she realised.

Jackson stared down at the little glass bottle. His eyes widened in shock and surprise.

Raraarg surged forwards. A glutinous hand snatched up the phial, holding it close to the Doctor's face as the slit-like mouth dribbled and spat. The creature's body shook with agitation.

'Where did it go?' the Doctor interpreted. 'Well, I would have thought that that was obvious.' He nodded towards the pale-looking Jackson. 'I put it in his tea.'

'All the time,' Jackson said quietly, in a voice that was somehow warmer and more emotional than before, 'every single moment, I knew what was happening. I tried to escape – to find ways out of the prison of my own mind. I managed to get control for long enough to transfer a tiny part of my own memory to Prisoner Nine. I hoped that way to warn you, Doctor. But it was like looking out through windows in my own head. Windows...' He looked at the Doctor. 'Of course, that's the answer. I remember what you said, Doctor. Thank you. And goodbye.'

'No!' the Doctor shouted. 'No, no, no – don't do that!'

He reached across the desk, trying to grab Jackson as the man rose to his feet.

Raraarg moved quickly, despite its bulk. The Doctor was knocked sideways as the creature surged forwards. Globby arms lashed out, sending Jackson flying sideways. He crashed to the floor.

'Hold on to something!' the Doctor shouted to Amy.

She grabbed the side of a bookcase, welded to the wall. 'Why?'

'Just hold on tight!'

Raraarg was bearing down on Jackson. The man pushed himself backwards, scrabbling for the Talerian gun knocked from his hands when he fell. He found it, brought it up, and fired.

Not at the alien creatures about to strike at him. At the wide picture window behind the desk.

The glass exploded into fragments, which were immediately whipped away as air rushed out of the base. An alarm sounded. The teacup and empty phial on the desk shot out of the window as the air escaped. Books were torn from the shelves, papers whipped into a swirling frenzy.

The Talerian leader gave an anguished cry of anger

and pain. Then it exploded like a balloon blown up too much. Glutinous, viscous fluid spattered across the room. The plates of armour went flying.

Amy's hair was blowing round her face as she held tight to the end of the bookcase, struggling to brace herself in position despite the wind trying to drag her towards the window.

Across the room, Jackson smiled with satisfaction. Then he was gone, his body tumbled across the grey lunar surface, debris and detritus from the base following.

'Decompression alert!' Captain Reeve yelled as the sirens went off. 'Hold on!'

'Get the door closed,' Carlisle ordered. 'It'll slow the loss of air.'

In the corridor, the Talerians were swept off their feet by the sudden rush of air drawn through the base. They tumbled backwards. As the pressure dropped, their bodies started to swell. Then, like their leader, they exploded – hurling grey-green ooze down the corridor.

'Oh gross!' Carlisle said. She gave the door a final heave shut.

Throughout Base Diana, the same thing was happening to all the Talerians. With the doors locked open, the whole base depressurised as the air escaped. Atmosphere pumps struggled to keep up. Emergency systems signalled bulkheads to close – with no effect, thanks to Major Carlisle's earlier sabotage.

In Jackson's office, the Doctor was holding on to

the edge of the heavy desk.

'Here – help me, Amy!' he yelled.

'I'm not letting go,' she shouted back.

But she was. She could feel her feet being dragged from under her. Fingers slipping on the metal.

'I'll catch you,' the Doctor promised.

She didn't have any choice. Amy's fingers finally lost their grip and she tumbled towards the window.

The Doctor's arm grabbed her as she flew past, dragging her down behind the desk.

The whole desk was shifting now, dragged towards the smashed window.

'We'll have to time this just right,' the Doctor shouted above the noise of the rushing air. He was holding tight to one of the two support struts holding up the desk.

Amy nodded. She realised now what he was going to do. She grabbed the other support strut. 'Count of three.'

The Doctor grinned. 'Three!' he yelled.

At the same moment, they each lifted and flipped the desk over on its side. Caught in the outrush, the desk flew across the room, top surface first. The desk was bigger than the window. It slammed over the hole, sealing it tight. The pressure held the desk incongruously in place, as if it had been glued to the wall.

The Doctor dusted his hands together. 'Result,' he said.

'One nil to the good guys,' Amy agreed, still gasping for breath. 'We should get to the canteen.'

The Doctor grinned. 'Just as soon as I've sealed

this room shut and turned off the homing beam that Jackson's equipment is broadcasting. Then, cinnamon buns here we come, oh yes indeed.'

Chapter
25

'Without the quantum link,' said General Walinski, 'Base Diana is unsustainable.'

'To be honest, I'm amazed it worked as long as it did,' the Doctor told him. 'The whole thing was incredibly unstable. Could have failed at any moment.'

The Doctor and Amy were in Walinski's office with Candace Hecker and Agent Jennings.

'You managed to get the quantum displacement systems working long enough for you and Miss Pond to get back, I see,' Agent Jennings said.

'Something like that,' Amy agreed.

'And Pat Ashton is due to splash down in a couple of hours,' Candace said. 'He's a bit low on oxygen, but he'll be fine.'

'We'll have to put together another mission to bring everyone back,' Walinski said. 'Shame they couldn't all come back with you.'

'They were a bit busy,' Amy said. 'We just snuck out.'

'Left them to tidy up, check the base is airtight again, do the washing up,' the Doctor said. 'Oh, and dismantle Jackson's equipment, too, before anyone gets the idea it can be salvaged and tries to get it working again.'

'So how do we get them back?' Jennings wanted to know.

'Can we rely on your help again, Doctor?' asked Candace.

'Oh you know what it's like – things to do, people to visit. Invading aliens to sort out. But I've got some notes you can have on how to adapt one of the decommissioned space shuttles for the flight to the moon. And I'll pop in if I get a chance.'

'Why do I feel that's a snub?' Candace said.

'You'll manage,' the Doctor told her. 'You'll do magnificently.'

'What are you going to do with the prisoners?' Amy asked. 'They don't deserve to be shipped off to another world like that. It's like deportation all over again.'

Jennings said: 'Most of them are due for release anyway under the President's new plans. It was Jackson's influence – or rather his alien counterpart's – that kept them up there. The others, well I'll make sure they're dealt with fairly. They'll be properly treated, I assure you.'

'They'd better be,' the Doctor said. 'I'll be watching.'

'I believe you, Doctor.'

'I know you want to be on your way,' Walinski said, 'and no doubt you have your own reports to write and forms to fill in.'

'No doubt,' the Doctor said.

'But we will need to debrief you both thoroughly. Could take a while, I'm afraid. And I think we all have some pretty searching questions. Obviously I'll clear it with your superiors. Which Agency did you say you were with again?'

The Doctor and Amy exchanged glances. 'Tell you what,' the Doctor said, 'why don't we get ourselves some coffee or something and we'll be right back.'

Jennings' mouth twitched into a smile beneath his ever-present dark-tinted glasses. 'No problem. I think we could all do with a short break.'

'Bye then,' Amy said. 'For now, I mean.'

'Yes,' the Doctor said. 'Bye for now. It's been... real.'

Candace got coffee for the others while they waited for the Doctor and Amy to return.

'So what's with that blue cupboard he had brought in?' Walinski asked.

'I didn't see it,' she admitted. 'But I did hear a funny noise – did you? Like a rasping, grating sound.'

'Sort of wheezing and groaning?' Walinski said. 'We heard that. I think it came from outside. There's a window open somewhere. It blew some papers across the office.'

'Except,' Agent Jennings said slowly, 'this is a secure building. None of the windows open.' He took his glasses off and gently rubbed the bridge of his nose where they had been resting. 'You know, I'm not sure we're going to see those two again.'

'What makes you say that?' Candace asked.

'Just a feeling,' he said. 'At the back of my mind.' He smiled suddenly. 'And I've read the UNIT files.'

It struck Candace that she'd never seen Agent Jennings' eyes before. She'd expected them to be as dark and colourless as the lenses of his glasses. But in fact they were a bright, cheerful green.

248

DOCTOR ░ WHO
Night of the Humans
by David Llewellyn

£6.99 ISBN 978 1 846 07969 6

250,000 years' worth of junk floating in deep space, home to the shipwrecked Sittuun, the carnivorous Sollogs, and worst of all – the Humans.

The Doctor and Amy arrive on this terrifying world in the middle of an all-out frontier war between Sittuun and Humans, and the clock is already ticking. There's a comet in the sky, and it's on a collision course with the Gyre…

When the Doctor is kidnapped, it's up to Amy and 'galaxy-famous swashbuckler' Dirk Slipstream to save the day.

But who is Slipstream, exactly? And what is he really doing here?

A thrilling, all-new adventure featuring the Doctor and Amy, as played by Matt Smith and Karen Gillan in the spectacular hit series from BBC Television.

Available now from BBC Books:

DOCTOR ⬚ WHO
The Forgotten Army
by Brian Minchin

£6.99 ISBN 978 1 846 07987 0

New York – one of the greatest cities on 21st century Earth... But what's going on in the Museum? And is that really a Woolly Mammoth rampaging down Broadway?

An ordinary day becomes a time of terror, as Ice Age creatures come back to life, and the Doctor and Amy meet a new and deadly enemy. The vicious Army of the Vykoid are armed to the teeth and determined to enslave the human race. Even though they're only three inches high.

With the Vykoid army swarming across Manhattan and sealing it from the world with a powerful alien forcefield, Amy has just 24 hours to find the Doctor and save the city. If she doesn't, the people of Manhattan will be taken to work in the doomed asteroid mines of the Vykoid home planet.

But as time starts to run out, who can she trust? And how far will she have to go to free New York from the Forgotten Army?

A thrilling, all-new adventure featuring the Doctor and Amy, as played by Matt Smith and Karen Gillan in the spectacular hit series from BBC Television.

Coming soon from BBC Books:

DOCTOR ⊙ WHO
The TARDIS Handbook
by Steve Tribe

£12.99 ISBN 978 1 846 07986 3

The inside scoop on 900 years of travel aboard the Doctor's famous time machine.

Everything you need to know about the TARDIS is here – where it came from, where it's been, how it works, and how it has changed since we first encountered it in that East London junkyard in 1963.

Including photographs, design drawings and concept artwork from different eras of the series, this handbook explores the ship's endless interior, looking inside its wardrobe and bedrooms, its power rooms and sick bay, its corridors and cloisters, and revealing just how the show's production teams have created the dimensionally transcendental police box, inside and out.

The TARDIS Handbook is the essential guide to the best ship in the universe.

Coming soon from BBC Books:

DOCTOR ⏻ WHO
Nuclear Time
by Oli Smith

£6.99 ISBN 978 1 846 07989 4

Colorado, 1981. The Doctor and Amy arrive in Appletown – an idyllic village in the remote American desert where the townsfolk go peacefully about their suburban routines. But when two more strangers arrive, things begin to change. The first is a mad scientist – whose warnings are cut short by an untimely and brutal death. The second is the Doctor...

As death falls from the sky, the Doctor is trapped. The TARDIS is damaged, and the Doctor finds he is living backwards through time. With Amy being hunted through the suburban streets of the Doctor's own future and getting farther away with every passing second, he must unravel the secrets of Appletown before time runs out...

A thrilling, all-new adventure featuring the Doctor and Amy, as played by Matt Smith and Karen Gillan in the spectacular hit series from BBC Television.

Coming soon from BBC Books:

DOCTOR ◉ WHO
The King's Dragon
by Una McCormack

£6.99   ISBN 978 1 846 07990 0

In the city-state of Geath, the King lives in a golden hall, and the people want for nothing. Everyone is happy and everyone is rich. Or so it seems.

When the Doctor and Amy look beneath the surface, they discover a city of secrets. In dark corners, strange creatures are stirring. At the heart of the hall, a great metal dragon oozes gold. Then the Herald appears, demanding the return of her treasure – the 'glamour'… And next come the gunships.

The battle for possession of the glamour has begun, and only the Doctor and Amy can save the people of the city from being destroyed in the crossfire of an ancient civil war.

But will the King surrender his new-found wealth? Or will he fight to keep it…?

A thrilling, all-new adventure featuring the Doctor and Amy, as played by Matt Smith and Karen Gillan in the spectacular hit series from BBC Television.